Other works by Michael Juge

RIDE THE WILDERNESS BOOK ONE OF THE SHIFT TRILOGY
2012   ★Previously released in 2010 as "Scourge of an Agnostic God"

A HARD RAIN BOOK TWO OF THE SHIFT TRILOGY
2012   ★First edition released in 2011

REFURBISHED SOUL BOOK THREE OF THE SHIFT TRILOGY
2012

Here We Are Now

A '90s Austin Story

MICHAEL JUGE

iUniverse LLC
Bloomington

HERE WE ARE NOW
A '90S AUSTIN STORY

iUniverse books may be ordered through booksellers or by contacting:

iUniverse
1663 Liberty Drive
Bloomington, IN 47403
www.iuniverse.com
1-800-Authors (1-800-288-4677)

ISBN: 978-1-4917-0200-0 (sc)
ISBN: 978-1-4917-0201-7 (hc)
ISBN: 978-1-4917-0202-4 (e)

Printed in the United States of America.

iUniverse rev. date: 08/06/2013

For my wife:
You know who you are.

Hey, reader! Thanks!

Dear reader,

Hi. I'm Michael Juge. If you purchased this novel by mistake thinking that I am that guy Mike Judge who created *Beavis and Butthead*, *King of the Hill* and other great comedies, you have my apologies. I can't tell you how many calls I've received from people over the years telling me what I brilliant writer I am. I was so flattered and emboldened by all the positive reinforcement only to later find out that these calls were from fans who thought they were calling Mike *Judge*. That being said, if you did purchase this knowing that I am not he, I tip my hat to you, sir or madam. I appreciate the opportunity to entertain you.

Sincerely,

Michael Juge

A note about the soundtrack to
Here We Are Now

My formative years were spent in the '80s. It was the decade that brought you the montage and perfected the original motion picture soundtrack (think "Eye of the Tiger"). As a result, I was reared with the idea that every great work should have accompanying music. Books were no exception. So, when I started producing my own novels, I decided to include a soundtrack to go with the narratives I created. Throughout this story, you will see an annotation in bold print that looks something like:

Song being overplayed on the radio:
"Doin' Time" by Sublime
Visit <u>www.michaeljuge.com</u> on the *Here We Are Now* page to listen

This is a prompt for you, the reader, to go to the website <u>www.michaeljuge.com</u> on the *Here We Are Now* page. Select the YouTube link of the referenced song (they're listed in the order in which they appear in the novel) and listen while you read so that you may enjoy the full sensory experience. If you would like to hear background music throughout the story, I suggest you tune your Internet radio station to either '90s alternative or Cake. One day, eReaders will be capable of playing a YouTube link while displaying the text. Unfortunately, that day is not yet here. Until then, you have my website to supplement this novel.

Prologue:
Nobody could have guessed that the universe was going to end on a Tuesday

Every generation has a story to tell. For my grandparents, it was growing up during the Great Depression only to come of age to fight in an earth-shattering world war. For my parents' generation it was Vietnam, the Civil Rights Movement and the cultural and social revolutions they participated in during the '60s. The Millennials came of age to endure 9/11, the Great Recession, the quagmires in Iraq and Afghanistan, and the three-ounce liquid limit through airport security. Sandwiched in between these massive generations is my own. Born between the advent of the birth control pill and advances in fertility treatments, we are the smallest in number. The marketing firms had difficulty defining this obscure segment of the population. Like brand X, we were something ill-defined and generic to them. We became known simply by the marketing term used to describe us: *Generation X.* So, what's our story?

We had Nirvana, the rise of the Internet and the Information Age and some minor military skirmishes, but nothing that our children will be forced to memorize in class. We had the whole Monica Lewinsky affair, Columbine, and angst-fueled music. We saw the birth of the startup, the transformation of alternative music from college radio to Clear Channel, and an explosion of wealth not seen since the waning days of the bubonic plague. That was the '90s in a nutshell, well that and the fact that the universe came within a breath of complete annihilation outside of a big box store. You probably don't remember that at all. That's the funny thing. Of all of the events of consequence that happened during the '90s, the decade when my generation flowered, the most critical one of them all, the very moment that defined reality itself occurred and nobody even knew about it. The only scraps of evidence that remain are the cached news agency Internet pages reporting a mass suicide at the Stubb Foundation.

The media of the time pitched the mass suicide as a dotcom that took the whole "drinking the Kool-Aid" trope a bit too literally. There was no suicide note left at the reception desk (there was no reception desk, or receptionist, actually), so people were left to come up with their own conclusions. Some claim that when the Stubb Foundation was about to go to its initial public offering, the employees agreed to commit suicide rather than face the inevitable collapse of the company. Others said that the mass suicide was simply a team building exercise taken too far. It was as good an explanation as any, given the times, and especially in a place like Austin where startups flourished in a consequence-free environment. Yet for all the speculation as to why they did it, nobody could figure out exactly what the Stubb Foundation did to make money. Of course, wasn't that the problem with most of the dotcoms of the time?

If anybody does recall the case of the dotcom suicide, they couldn't know what really happened, what the Stubb Foundation's true mission was and how it saved the totality of all existence from total collapse. Nobody knew that little spicy nugget of trivia except me. The only reason I know the truth is simple: I just happened to be "the Chris." But I'm getting ahead of myself.

1

Where the weird things are

November 1996

Question: How many Austinites does it take to screw in a light bulb?
Answer: Three. One to replace the light bulb and two to reminisce
           about the old one and how much better it all was before it
           got commercial.

Austin, Texas is hard to describe. Topographically, the city straddles
the Hill Country on the western half and the terrace to the east. Bio
regionally, it straddles the forest to its east, the plains to its north and the
semi-arid savannah to its west. Politically, Austin is a stridently liberal
city in an otherwise conservative state. In other words, Austin is weird.
It's proud of the green spaces that it painstakingly preserved, including
the crown jewel of the Greenbelt, and jealously protects its local
businesses and landmarks from the ever-encroaching homogenization
metastasizing in the rest of the country. Austinites are by and large
educated, liberal, outdoorsy and by city ordinance they all wear earth
tones. Austinites love to make fun of Dallas, Houston and LA, but they
show a particular deference for their Latino brethren an hour south in
San Antonio. It's the kind of place that drew people to California decades
ago. In fact, the only thing keeping the entire state of California from
moving to Austin is that it is hot as shit (hot as shit being technically
determined to be between 103 and 112 degrees. Anything above 112

1

degrees is hotter than f&*k, below 103 degrees but above 95 degrees is hot as balls).

Another thing about Austinites: They absolutely hate it whenever their city gets mentioned in the news. Whenever MSN has one of those top places to live, top cities to find work, top cities for quality of life, Austin ranks up in the top ten, if not the top five. Austinites can't stand that for they do not want you to know just how awesome living in Austin is. And they have a point. Austin is weird to be certain, but nine out of ten dentists agree that Austin used to be even weirder. As more people moved to Austin to experience the weird, the increase in intentional weirdness actually disrupted the fragile ecological balance, reducing its authentic quirkiness. Newly erected ice houses and cigar bars, painstakingly designed to look run down and gritty, began to pop up. I would one day call this architectural style "contrived authenticity." ™ Then again, that's a typical Austin thing to do, pine over the past, lament the city's incredible success and talk about how great it used to be before everyone moved there (especially the damned Californians). That's exactly what I did about six months after moving to Austin in autumn 1996, which is arguably the last moments before Austin became a real city.

Song on the car radio: "Where It's At" by Beck
Visit <u>www.michaeljuge.com</u> on the *Here We Are Now* page to listen

I fell for Austin from the moment I drove into the city and pulled up to Espresso Lube—a coffeehouse/auto mechanic shop. The sign outside advertised, "If it's in stock, we got it." It took me several seconds to get the snarky humor, for I came from the swamps of New Orleans.

The two cities had a couple of things in common: They were both liberal islands in red states and each had its own unique heritage, which they actively loved and guarded from being overtaken by national chains.

But where New Orleans was a city in a constant state of decay, both in terms of its economic prospects and its physical infrastructure, Austin was blooming with vitality. New Orleans was home to gutter punks, homeless runaways who thought Mardi Gras was a year-round thing and yats while Austin was home to proto-hipsters, homeless runaways who thought that South By Southwest was a year-round thing, graphic designers and software engineers. Where New Orleans' economy was based on tourism, Austin's was based on high-tech business. Where New Orleans was the murder capital, Austin was the live music capital. New Orleans had awesome mosh funk and brass hop, Austin had awesome alt country and post punk. New Orleans had thousand-year-old oak trees that canopy the city. Austin had a mixture of diminutive oaks and cactuses. While New Orleans, already several feet below sea level, was slowly sinking further into the Gulf, Austin was a hilly city with vistas that overlooked the Hill Country. You get the idea.

It wasn't hard for me to leave everything behind back then. I was single and everything I owned fit inside my Toyota pickup truck's bed: my clothes, my TV/VCR combo with all of my *X-Files* VHS tapes, my cassettes and CDs, a futon mattress and my new Kona mountain bike, which I got as a graduation present. I sold my bass guitar, because I heard Austin had little use for another bass player. Besides, it had bad juju attached to it. My truck was easy to recognize. The blue 1986 compact pickup had one distinctive item that distinguished it from the millions of other Toyota pickups on the road. There was a gigantic sticker, the width of the truck itself, that advertised, "Value Menus." Friends of mine stole it from a Taco Bell back in 1991 and placed it on my truck's lift gate while I was passed out. That was back before I got sober (which is a whole different story for another time). Anyway, I reckoned the "Value Menus" sticker a good thing, so I kept it. *Value Menus*, which became the christened name of my pickup, has served me well ever since.

My friend Stacy took me in upon puttering into town on a random Tuesday evening. We met back in New Orleans when I first got sober in '94. She had a year sobriety at the time while I had three months, and she could tell I was treading dangerously close to a relapse. She befriended me and we hung out with a bunch of sober punks who committed harmless felonies on what was the wild Internet back then. Stacy was a transient type. She claimed to originally be from Stockdale, Arizona, though I can't corroborate that. I never met any of her family.

Her skin was a bit leathery for someone in her twenties, but she had a seductive raspy smoker's voice and she didn't overdo it with the skin ink. I was smitten with her at first, I'll admit, but after spending a couple of months with her, I was glad to be one of her friends and not one of her boyfriends.

That summer back in '94, Stacy introduced me to this new Internet thing. I watched her hack into the mainframes of banks, airlines and a few government agencies just for the hell of it. I was scared shitless that we'd get arrested, but she reminded me that I had nothing to worry about. I didn't know how to get online, much less hack anything. She was right. I didn't learn a damned thing computer-wise from her. But I did learn about staying up past 3 a.m. every night completely sober, doing shots of espresso and smoking profusely. Stacy left New Orleans at the end of that summer to move to Austin for no particular reason while I returned to school to finish my degree.

I hadn't intended to ever leave my home. I just wasn't the type to leave New Orleans. Most New Orleanians aren't. Besides, I had a good thing going where I was. I had a great sponsor in AA, a guy named Aidan, a jaded Vietnam veteran who regaled me with tales of being in "the shit" and skillfully tied his war stories with me staying sober. I was a bass player in a funk band called Senator Monkey and the Funkicrats. We weren't headliners yet, but we were gaining a decent following. I even had a girlfriend. I was generally content. I would have never left, but two years later, a few months after obtaining my bachelors in philosophy, Fate intervened. Specifically, I found Fate, the lead singer of our band, in bed with my girlfriend. The next day, my mediocre bassist skills were replaced by some mouth breather whose one claim to fame was that he once stood in for the bass player of the Meteors. So, there I was: a fat, white dude with a useless degree in philosophy, no band, no girlfriend, and no longer with the delusion of becoming a breakout success.

I was slinging coffee at The Nervous Squirrel, an espresso bar downstairs from Mushroom Records near campus, trying not to get consumed by my recent turn of fortune. I lit a cigarette that had accidentally been dipped in a viscous, highly sweetened coffee called a Venetian cream before it dried out. The guy who made the Venetian cream concoction sold it to the espresso bar in these vats and he never provided us the formula which gave it its distinct flavor. All I knew was that the guy lived in an undisclosed location somewhere on the north shore, orders were left with an answering service and he demanded that we pay in cash. Weird. The university students drank it up like crazy during finals and before heading off to raves. I remember the moment well. I was slicing a bagel and inhaled the Venetian cream-saturated cigarette. Somebody spoke and then suddenly there was a flash and I had a vision. I didn't see a Native American in traditional garb with feathers as I'd often hoped I would see were I ever to receive a vision. Instead I had a vision of my future. It involved me moving back into my mom's house, getting a Nintendo and continuing to work at the espresso bar as the students seemed to get younger around me. I saw myself sitting on my mom's couch, getting fatter while watching *The X-Files* and coming up with new and exciting ways to make Prego a truly international sauce. The years seemed to pass by in seconds. I saw myself in the espresso bar now owned by someone else. I was wearing an ill-fitting T-shirt with the words "Worst sequel ever" printed in bold and I served kids espresso drinks with an acerbic attitude as I rambled on about once being in some band no one ever heard of. My transformation into a *Simpsons* character was complete. I awoke from the vision and felt this animalistic urge to flee.

I drove around town that evening weighing my options. The fact was that I didn't have a clue what to do now that I had graduated. I had been relying on the slim hope that Senator Monkey and the Funkicrats would get discovered. Now that I was out of the band, reality bitch-slapped me into what I believe psychiatrists called a panic-induced fugue. The good news about not having many options is that I didn't waste much gas on my drive. Upon returning to my apartment, I saw a message blinking on the answering machine (see pre-cell phone reference). It was my old friend Stacy from back in the summer of '94. She said she had been thinking about me. I quickly called her back, and we talked for hours. The next thing I knew, I was driving *Value Menus* to Austin and toward a path I hoped would not resemble anything like that vision I had from the Venetian cream clickum I smoked.

Stacy was staying at the Harvest Moon Co-op near the University of Texas campus in the center of town. The co-op had overtaken a once-proud fifteen-bedroom Victorian on Pearl Street. The thing about co-ops is this: They're kind of like temporary cults. The co-ops in Austin were concentrated around the UT campus, which made sense. Only the young could deal with the bullshit of living in such a setting. It's like voluntarily surrendering your privacy and hygiene for the illusion of camaraderie. But it wasn't camaraderie. It was being a bunch of young, poor-assed people willing to live in abject poverty around each other, but without quite slipping all the way into the crevice and staying at the Y.

The rent at the Harvest Moon Co-op didn't only go to pay for lodging and utilities; it went for food as well. Unfortunately, Stacy chose to live at a vegan co-op. There was a Straight Edge co-op down the block, and you would think that would be perfect for Stacy, right? She's a sober punk, after all. But like me, Stacy smoked like a chimney, hence her leathery skin and sexy raspy voice. She was only three years older than my 23, but she looked closer to 30. Stacy smoked, so the Straight Edge house was a no-go. Stacy wasn't a vegan either—she wasn't even a vegetarian, but the rent was reasonable and one of the residents at the house was also in recovery. Although not a proper vegetarian, Stacy was fine living in a vegan house. She cooked and ate vegan meals, and she more or less lived her life unaffected by her housemates, paying extra for the penthouse suite. She had a real job as a web designer whereas the others were students.

So, I rolled up in *Value Menus* on a Tuesday evening. It was a few nights after that *X-Files* episode aired documenting the journey of the cigarette-smoking man from an idealistic young operative to the nefarious murdering hatchet man he became. Stacy looked great. I couldn't say the same for myself. I had gained some weight since we last saw each other. I wasn't exactly obese like one of those people that get caught on TV with their faces blurred to report on the evils of corn syrup, but I could comfortably say that I was a card-carrying fat guy. You'd think that getting sober would help, but in sobriety I discovered how tasty food was.

Stacy helped me move my things into her suite and I had my own little nook in the corner. She was dating some random guy who worked at the Central Market—I've long since forgotten the guy's name. All I knew was that he turned me off to blonde dreadlocks. I stayed in Stacy's suite for weeks while I looked for work. The first couple of weeks in Austin were fun. I had built up a little bit of a financial cushion so I wasn't desperate just yet.

2

To be young and underpaid

1997

Song on my mixtape of job-seeking ennui:
"Sour Times" by Portishead
Visit **www.michaeljuge.com** on the *Here We Are Now* page to listen

Several weeks went by with no luck in the job search. At first I chalked it up to it being the holidays. That seemed reasonable enough; however, this was Austin in the '90s. The economy was absolutely exploding with jobs. But to be more precise, it was exploding with high-tech jobs. That's a wonderful thing if you are conversant in HTML or can at least bullshit your way through an interview about knowledge of some software they just hadn't heard of yet. But I had this dirty little secret. I never learned computers. Even as late as 1996 I typed my senior thesis about nihilism as expressed in *Pulp Fiction* on an electric type writer, because, and I quote myself, "I don't trust typing something down and I don't see it on paper right then and there." God, I was such a tool.

I sort of played it fast and loose around my schoolmates pretending I knew what they were talking about when they spoke about the release of Windows 95 being the greatest thing on earth. Stacy, on the other hand, was a certified hacker. She tried to teach me a few times, but it always ended up with me curled up on the floor in a fetal position when I hit the wrong key, which invariably lost my data. So, to recap: I was

8

a fat white guy with a degree in philosophy who had an irrational fear of computers in the Silicon Valley of the Southwest.

I combed the classifieds and applied to numerous companies with names like Aries 9, Tivoli, Oracle, The Rancorp, and Hoovers. Dell had its own employment page in the Austin American Statesman. I sent my resume to all of them and heard back from not one of them. But tucked away at the bottom of the classifieds, there was one ad seeking a "manager trainee" at a place called Terminal Car Rentals.

No experience necessary, no skills required. Just
a college degree and a willingness.

"A willingness?" *For what?* I thought their ad to be vague but I was in no position to be picky. I drove over to Terminal Car Rentals by Robert Mueller Airport to fill out an application. A harried-looking young lady behind the counter about my age gave me a glance when I told her I was interested in applying for the job opening. I couldn't describe the look. It was a cross between sympathy and utter despondency. At the time, however, I just took her words, "It's your funeral," as she handed me the application as a sign of encouragement.

I got the call the next day and I was hired as a manager trainee. They hired anyone who could string a sentence together, and they absolutely didn't give a shit about their employees, their cars or their reputation. They're still in business to this day, by the way. In fact, they have expanded nationally. I guess that's the unseen hand of the market at work.

I was paid two dollars over minimum wage, and was scheduled to work 50 hours while being paid for 40 hours. They could justify doing that because I was a manager trainee. I don't know if that was legal, but again . . . not in the position to argue. I had to wear golf shirts and pleated pants. Nothing accentuates fat like pleated pants. Meanwhile, Stacy got another job at a new company called CynerDygm. Pronounce that "sinner dime," as in "synergy" and "paradigm." CynerDygm was the merger of two dotcoms: Cynergy and Paradigm. I didn't know startups merged, but word had it that Cynergy was developing enterprise application software for Oracle and Paradigm had this awesome built-in bar, so it was a natural fit. Stacy's experience in breaking into Shell Oil, the Heritage Foundation and the US Department of Agriculture's mainframes to put pot leaves and rainbow flags on their websites finally paid off. She was hired as a web designer.

The only problem was that she didn't have a car and was stuck with a $1,000 credit limit, which was almost maxed out. CynerDygm was located out in the west hills off the Capital of Texas Highway also known as the 360. Suffice it to say, it wasn't walking distance from campus and as progressive as Austin was, it was still in Texas, so public transportation wasn't a realistic option. So, I lent Stacy *Value Menus* while I cycled to Terminal Car Rentals on my brand new Kona mountain bike.

Every day I cycled up and down hills from the Harvest Moon Co-op on the west side of campus up Guadalupe, then headed east under the I-35 to Manor Road and up and down more hills all the way to work. I'm a sweater. I don't mean to say that I'm a garment to be worn when you're chilly. I mean I perspire. I sweat when I exercise. I sweat when I'm trying on clothes at the mall. I sweat when I eat. "Yeah, all fat people do that, Chris," you might say, but eventually I got thin . . . well, okay, not Willem Dafoe thin, but thinner. I was thin enough to be not noticeably overweight with a shirt on, and I still sweated like someone seeing their ex-lover testify at a Senate confirmation hearing. I didn't get that heroin chic look with abs of Jesus thing, but in eight months I went from wearing 42s to wearing 36s, although when I sat down the waistband of the 36s had its tensile strength severely tested. It was the cycling that did it.

At first it was kind of frightening, because I was not particularly practiced cycling on city streets, and the service road of the I-35 is dangerous business in a car and damned near suicidal on a bike. But I did it. Of course, I quickly learned not to cycle to work wearing my work clothes. There's nothing more unappealing than renting a jalopy from a dude with fresh sweat under his arms, cascading down his back to his ass, which is very apparent in pleated khakis. So, I changed at work and discovered why everyone wore patchouli. It really does cover body odor well. Good find, hippies.

While Stacy was living it up like a pimp as a web designer, I was hacking it at Terminal Car Rentals. Our hours often conflicted, but whenever we got the chance, Stacy and I would go out to AA meetings together. She dumped blonde dreadlocks guy within a month of me moving in. Apparently, he was too conservative. He had a hang up about making sweet love while I lounged in the corner eating a bucket of fried chicken watching *The X-Files*. Hey, I wore headphones. Oh, and you might have noticed, I was eating fried chicken at a vegan co-op. More on that later.

Everyone had these dreams of moving to Austin, where you would chill in Barton Creek during the day, go to Liberty Lunch at night and work at a coffeehouse in between which somehow took care of all of your living expenses. Okay, not everyone. I had these dreams. Anyway, it turned out that none of the good coffeehouses were hiring, I had no practical skills like plumbing or electrical engineering, and everyone else demanded a basic understanding of computers.

My first day at Terminal went something like this: The daytime manager, who was the nephew of the owner, Jebediah Orwell, took me outside of the modular facility of Terminal. The yard where the fleet of vehicles was kept was a barren dirt field speckled with a few sprouts of grass competing for water with a couple of sad-looking cactuses. Chickens freely roamed the yard while an attendant shooed away a rooster making it with a hen inside one of the vehicles to be rented out.

"You see those Oldsmobiles there?"

"The ones with smoke coming out of the hoods?"

"Yeah, them. They just came in from our San Antonio office. Get them cleaned up and ready to be rented out. We call them full size 'cause they've got a tape deck and a moon roof."

I spent those days renting out these Detroit abortions to people who flew in from places like San Angelo and Lubbock. None of our customers had the proper credit to rent from a respectable rental car company. We were their only hope. I'd rent out these Oldsmobile Sierras and Buick Centurys which hadn't been redesigned since Lee Iacocca's heyday. Without fail, the customers would call within hours complaining, "My rental smells funny," "My rental shakes and shimmies whenever I go over 50," "My rental broke down. I don't know where I am and I hear wolves howling." Ten hours a day inside a prefab modular facility calling towing companies, taking complaints, and frantically trying to scrounge more vehicles because the reservations department had no concept of inventory was standard practice at Terminal. We did our best to clean our shoes of chicken droppings whenever we entered the building, but the place reeked of digested corn. This was no way to become part of Austin.

There wasn't any place to eat nearby except this roach coach that doubled as a pharmaceutical outlet selling pot. I'll say they did have great breakfast tacos. In fact, Midnight Tacos was famous for their breakfast tacos . . . well, that and their pot. They were raking in the cash until they got busted precisely because of their fame for reasonably priced pot. It's a difficult business model, I suppose. I was always too stressed out to eat more than one or two tacos during my shift. People yelling, cursing me out and calling me an asshole for not being cool after they returned a car with fresh collision marks had a way of sapping my appetite. On the upside, between the sparse eating and the constant cycling, I quickly lost weight.

Another upside: Unlike every other rental car company, Terminal didn't have computers. Jebediah Orwell, the owner of the thriving rent-a-wreck, had a thing against them. He contended that one day computers would all be controlled by the UN. He sent memos about dress code or about our non-existent sick leave policy, and on the bottom of each memo was a scrawling that displayed the birthmark he claimed that Bill Clinton had, which was the mark of Satan. Jebediah came in from time to time and told me to not drink anything but rainwater and unpasteurized milk.

I lived my life at Terminal Car Rentals, and I hated it. I woke up some mornings from these nightmares. Some were work anxiety dreams. I'd wake up answering, "Terminal Car Rentals. Can I help you?" Others were variations on the Venetian cream vision I had at the espresso bar. Stacy was my only outlet to the outside world. I would cycle home sometime after eleven at night and I picked up a couple of burgers at one of the college bars along the way.

We had a system living at the vegan co-op to deal with our carnivorous ways. We would eat the burgers or fried chicken, place the soiled wrappers and napkins in a Ziploc plastic bag, thoroughly wash with Lava soap and spritz the place with patchouli. Again, good find, hippies. The next morning Stacy would take the evidence out and dispose of it in the frat house's garbage next door. Eventually, I took up more permanent residence in the neighboring room, much to our mutual relief.

3

Pimp of the year

1997

I met Raquel on the night Fox aired the *X-Files* episode about Assistant Director Skinner having a one-night stand with a woman who wound up dead next to him. One of the advantages Terminal Car Rentals had over the competition was that it rented to people under 25. Raquel's car was in the shop and being 24 she found herself renting from us. Raquel stood out from the regulars in line with her curly blonde hair, big blue eyes and skin-tight jeans. I lucked out and got to her rather than my co-worker Chad. Raquel was kind of loud and had a yat-like accent, so I asked if she happened to be from New Orleans. She said she wasn't. She was from Houston like half the city of Austin was, but she liked that I was from there and said I had *chutzpah*. She took the keys and thanked me. I thought that was it and resumed serving the rest of the extras from the Mos Eisley Cantina.

It was well after eleven when I closed up shop for the evening. I believed I had shed roughly five pounds in water weight that day along with the remaining vestiges of my Locke-centered view of humanity. It had been a long day and I just wanted to go home, eat a bucket of contraband fried chicken and pass out. I mounted my Kona and was about to pull out onto the street when I saw Raquel leaning against the Oldsmobile rental. I swear she made that piece of shit Cierra look sexy.

"Hey, Nawlins' boy! You up for a beer?" She called out in her naturally loud voice.

Now, here's the thing.

One: Girls don't pick up on me.

Two: I'm sober. She asked if I wanted to go for a beer. I don't drink.

So, the question was, what do I say?

"Um, I don't drink." *Idiot! You could have said "sure" and just not gotten a beer when you got to wherever she's inviting you. Moron! Worst response . . .*

"Is it a religious thing?" she interrupted my concentrated efforts at self-flagellation.

"Oh God, no! No. It's just . . . I can go out for a beer, but I'll have a Coke."

"Sober boy. Even better." She gestured at my bike. "That your ride?"

Song being played at the coffeehouse: "6 Underground" by Sneaker Pimps
Visit <u>www.michaeljuge.com</u> on the *Here We Are Now* page to listen

Raquel and I went to this coffeehouse/laundromat off of Duval in Hyde Park that had live music where we chatted and got to know each other. I was on my third iced coffee, so I could get my liquid courage on, but it tended to make me talk even more. Some women prefer that dark, brooding, mysterious, quiet type. I'm kind of the opposite. In fact, I'm sort of like the pasty, babbling and obvious type. But that didn't seem to bother Raquel. In fact, she was weird. She was a beautiful lady who turned heads wherever she passed by, but she wasn't full of herself. She also had a tendency to fart, saying that it was a byproduct of her forced vegetarianism.

"Why forced?" I asked as she let one out.

"I'm an exotic dancer."

"Oh, like belly dancing. You work over at The Maghrib Lounge?"

She smacked me on the head. "No, dummy. It's a polite way of saying I'm a stripper."

"Oh." I was embarrassed. Not because she was a stripper, but because I totally didn't get the "exotic" reference.

Okay. Raquel was a stripper who wore skin-tight jeans and stilettos and she farted in public sometimes and blamed me when people turned around. She got her bachelor's in English Literature; therefore, she started stripping at Expose, where all the other English Lit graduates who wanted to stay in Austin worked. But she was also working on her master's degree in Middle Eastern Studies. She spoke Hebrew fluently and was currently taking Arabic. This kind of thing was actually commonplace in Austin: meeting highly educated strippers, gas station attendants and even car rental manager trainees. It's a city supersaturated with young people who came from all over who didn't want to leave after graduating, so they stayed and took whatever jobs they could get.

Raquel drove a Firebird which had these woofers that I always berated others for having—she claimed it really brought out Enya's voice. She was really . . . well, you know, passionate. But there was more to it than that. She did things for me. For instance, my 42s were now loose and I was cinching them together without any consideration as to how it looked. She noticed my ill-fitting clothes and got me pants that fit. They were 38s, if you were wondering. And they looked good on me. She also introduced me to boxer briefs. When everyone thinks of inventions from the '90s, they think of the Internet, Auto-Tune or the revolutionary speed of computer advancements. That's great and all, no doubt. Certainly, we wouldn't be where we are without that. But the advent of boxer briefs was mind blowing. Think about it. They provided the security of briefs without having to choose between cheesy banana hammocks, boxers with no security at all or pitiful diaper-looking rags that mirrored the same pair of underwear you had worn since you were four years old and made accidental skid marks. Boxer briefs maybe the most underrated invention of the '90s.

But along with flat front slacks, dark jeans and stylish boxer briefs, Raquel exposed me to Austin. As she was finishing up with her MA in Middle Eastern Studies, she often met with her colleagues at under-the-radar local coffeehouses and lounges to study. Raquel introduced me to all kinds of oddball clubs and hangouts tucked away in South Austin. Her friends included a wide array of fellow English Lit strippers, bouncers, Middle Eastern Studies classmates, an assortment of ancient hippies, which were required to be present by city ordinance at a meeting consisting of more than five people, and even a cadre of blacksmiths. I didn't even know one could make a living as a blacksmith. Raquel liked the fact that I didn't drink. It was sort of novel. She would pick me up after work, and it was so empowering seeing this beautiful, buxom blonde pulling up in a Firebird to pick me up. That won me major street cred with the guys at Terminal Car Rentals. I was pimp of the year to them as I stuffed my Kona mountain bike in the back of the Firebird.

It didn't last. After eight weeks, Raquel let me go. I wasn't crushed, really. She never got into *The X-Files* no matter how many hours I played for her, and she was a bit pushy and rude sometimes. But I'm not going to lie; it wasn't me who ended it. She did. Naturally, the first thing I asked was if it was the sex. That's what insecure white boys do. She laughed and assured me that I was quite proficient if a bit quick on the draw.

"So, what is it," I asked.

"Well, dude," she called me dude, which should tell you something, "you're just too clingy. You need to make more friends."

She wasn't wrong. She was the best thing to happen to me since arriving in Austin. I knew I wasn't in love with her; it was really just a physical thing. But I really, seriously did *not* want that physical thing to end. Oh well. It was a fantastic eight weeks.

Raquel left me much better off than when she found me, for along with ending an epic dry spell and introducing me to modern underpants, she gave me confidence to move on with things. What's more, she introduced me to the HR director at Logos Office Solutions, who hooked me up with a job that got me out of the purgatory that was Terminal Car Rentals. Raquel set things in motion. That intricate tapestry of life thing we hear so much about? Well, I see this passing interlude with Raquel as being a critical set of stitches in that tapestry.

Helpful hints about Austin: Part I

-Don't go to Hippie Hollow. It sounds like a fun place, a clothing optional beach on the opposite side of Mansfield Dam on Lake Travis. But you're not, I repeat, NOT going to see a bunch of UT cuties sunbathing naked. Instead you're going to be surrounded by a bunch of other pervs, naked post-middle aged dudes with bikini-waxed junk out in the open.

-Mountain Biking: The motocross trail at Emma Long Park is completely and utterly insane. Don't even think that you won't be carrying your bike most of the time. The descriptions in the biking guides say it's challenging. No. Challenging is trying to teach inner city kids the value of learning Shakespeare. This trail will break you.

-You want breakfast tacos on a weekend in a timely manner? You can scratch Kerbey Lane and Magnolia Café off your list. Great places, but unfortunately, everybody knows it.

-And speaking of breakfast tacos . . . if you happen to find a great place for breakfast tacos, don't tell anybody about it. Selfishly guard that secret and keep it to yourself like you would the location of a fallout shelter you had built and it's October 1962.

-Interstate 35 entrances: The original designers of the I-35 were pathological misanthropes who wanted to create chaos, fear and aggression as evidenced by the freeway entrances they developed. You are given roughly twenty feet from entering the freeway to the end of the merger. This causes a lot of people to panic and stop, backing up traffic for miles. My only advice for these ridiculously short entrances is to not look back and to just gun it. As they always say: The best defense is a good offense.

4

Welcome to the Lord of the Flies

1997

Raquel did me a real solid by connecting me with a friend in HR at Logos Office Solutions. I hoped I would be doing something office-like, managing things and going to business lunches with people who had cell phones, something befitting my bachelor's degree in philosophy. But then I was given a placement test on my computer skills. I have to say Microsoft Office in the Windows 95 era wasn't exactly user-friendly for the newly initiated. In any case, after once again being torpedoed by my peculiar computer impediment, I was assigned to be a courier, specifically a bike messenger. I had been cycling back and forth from the Harvest Moon Co-op to Terminal Car Rentals at the Robert Mueller Airport for months. So at least I could say I was in physical shape to take on the task.

Stacy tried to cheer me up. "Wow, you're now just like Puck!" (See MTV's third season of *The Real World* for the pop cultural reference)

"Ha ha," I responded mordantly.

We were sitting outside on the porch over at Flight Path Coffeehouse. The coffee was decent. Stacy really liked Flight Path because it had telephone outlets where she could connect to the Internet with an Ethernet cable. That was pretty neat. I wondered what they would think of next. Stacy had quit CynerDygm and was doing freelance work for a search engine company called Alta Vista on something called "search engine optimization." This was before Google took over the Internet. Back then, there were all sorts of search engines: Yahoo, AOL, Alta Vista . . . I forget the rest—I would have to Google it. As a freelancer she had no real office space. She spent a lot of her day working from a coffeehouse.

"Oh come, on, Chris. I think it's great. You get to work regular hours. In addition, you're paid for the hours you've worked. That's more than I can say, and plus you aren't stuck sitting down and getting flabby like me."

Stacy was always fishing for compliments. She was skinny and she knew it, so I didn't bother. But what she said made some sense. Besides, I would be downtown, not stuck on the eastside. And being a bike messenger couldn't be all that bad.

Song getting a lot of airplay:
"Sonny Came Home" by Shawn Colvin
Visit **www.michaeljuge.com** on the *Here We Are Now* page to listen

Logos Office Solutions was a company that contracted office management support to its clients. Let's say an office didn't want to have to worry about keeping its Xerox serviced, but it needed to make copies. It needed couriers to deliver documents to courthouses and other businesses but didn't want to get bogged down by invoices. Logos offered to manage business operations on a contract basis.

I was issued a beeper and I showed up to one of the client law offices' copy room where I found a group of smelly young men lounging by an array of Xerox and fax machines. Most of them had scabs on their knees and elbows. There was no uniform, yet all had this uncanny likeness about them, a dirty, raggedy look. The guys gave me a once-over.

"College boy," I heard one of them mumble.

The first guy I met was probably the most presentable of the bunch. He had bathed recently. He sauntered up to me and sized me up.

"You the new guy, ese?"

I nodded. Next to him was a tall, lanky guy who sat atop of one of the tables that held the mail slots.

"I'm Zeke. And baboso here's Reagan."

Reagan nodded, "Sup."

Zeke showed me around the office and I followed him the first half of the day where I met several other bike messengers from other companies. When he caught sight of my Kona mountain bike, Zeke scoffed.

"That's a mighty purty bike you got there, ese."

"Ah, thanks!"

It took me a couple of seconds to realize that it was a back-handed compliment. The guys rode bikes that were functional but ugly as hell. Most of the bikes' frames were wrapped in duct tape specifically to make them even more unappealing and therefore less tempting to a potential thief. Whereas my Kona was a proper mountain bike designed to handle rocky terrain, those who had mountain bikes modified them with street wheels. Cages, chains and spare tubes adorned the frames in a way that bespoke of Stalinesque utilitarianism. They displayed their political and band loyalties on their messenger bags.

Zeke and I got acquainted the usual way—through answering the most relevant question to someone in his early twenties. "What do you listen to?" Zeke was into third coast hip hop, guys like Mystikal and Master P. He was a little standoffish, but he showed me around and gave me a lot of helpful hints about saving time in deliveries.

On my first few days, I rode from campus to downtown, around downtown up past campus, back down Guadalupe to the south side of Town Lake, which was actually a river and has since been renamed Lady Bird Lake, and back up to the Capitol, and then to the Travis County Courthouse and back east again. It was late spring, but in typical Texas fashion, it was in the 90s. I was humping it all over town, and the thought entered my mind that I would be dead of a heat stroke come August. I managed to rip the crotch of two pairs of pants and permanently stain my shirts with sweat in a matter of two weeks.

I soon learned that the copy room at the Law Office of Taylor, Swift and Lavigne where I was assigned along with Zeke and Reagan was the congregation site for the Logos bike messengers. I tried to make conversation with the guys as we farted around the room sorting mail.

"Anybody watch that episode of *X-Files* last week?"

They just sort of ignored the question while Reagan continued with his story.

"So, I was banging this chick, right? And dude, I'm totally wasted. I finally cum, and she wants to sleep over."

"Man, I hate that shit," one of the guys opined.

"Yeah, so I send . . . whatever her name is to go get some more beer. And when she leaves, I took the phone off the hook so she can't get in the gate!"

All the guys laughed and slapped Reagan on the back. I couldn't help but cringe.

"Man, why would you do that?" I asked.

"What do I care? I don't know her."

"I don't know. It seems kind of a shitty thing to do."

"Oh lookie here. We got Mr. Alanis Morrisette on his pedestal," he chided.

We exchanged a few words when Zeke got between us. He put his arm around me to get me out of Reagan's way and said, "Don't pay any attention to him, Chris. The only reason that pendejo kicks the ladies out is because he doesn't want to hear what a lousy lay he is."

A little laughter.

"That's not what you mother says, *cabron*" Reagan retorted with his thick East Texas accent, butchering the Mexican slang.

More cackles. Zeke flips him the bird, "Fuck you, man."

I felt like I was transported back into fourth grade, complete with jibes about mothers. It went like that the first month or so. During that time, I hung out with Zeke a lot after work and got to know him and his girlfriend Laura and soon enough considered him to be a good friend. The rest were exactly like you would expect of a group of young men who were stuck around each other, breathing in each other's testosterone and encouraging each other. *Lord of the Flies*? That would totally happen. Sadly, I know which character I would be and who Reagan would be.

Reagan and I butted heads a lot in the beginning. I saw him as some raging racist misogynist. He saw me as some prissy know-it-all. I think we both were onto something. Our conversations always ended with me saying, "God, Reagan. You're such an asshole!" followed by his brilliant retort "That's what your mother says." He repeated that one-liner at least five times a day, and it never failed to get a laugh.

Things might have not have improved between us until this one time, Reagan was cycling down Congress Avenue and was turning left onto 4th Street into oncoming traffic. A car tagged his back wheel and he flipped over. I was heading up Congress at the very moment it happened and was stunned to see the car drive casually up the street after striking him. I raced as hard as my husky frame ever pedaled in my entire life. I don't know what got into me. I guess it was just that it could have easily been me to get tagged. I jumped a curb and got ahead of the driver and stopped right in his path. I was taking a chance, I know, relying on the social contract as I was betting that the driver wouldn't plow over me in broad daylight. It was a good gamble, for he stopped and waited for the police to arrive.

Reagan's bike was cashed, but he was unharmed other than a gash on his elbow and his knee, which was a bloody mess, another scab to add onto arms and legs full of them. He was well enough, in fact, that I had to hold him back from pummeling the driver. Afterwards, I supported Reagan's weight as he placed his arm over my shoulder and walked him back to the office. He didn't say anything in particular, but I noticed that his attitude towards me changed after that event. He stopped making jokes at my expense other than the typical guy banter, and he started inviting me to join the other guys to go out with them. Of course, when I took them to Expose, a gentleman's club employing English Lit graduates, and introduced the guys to some of Raquel's co-workers, that's when I officially became one of them. Male bonding sometimes involves common conflict, or facing a common challenge. But when a man buys another man a lap dance, it's his way of saying, "You're good people."

At some point I said, "Dude. It's like the *Lord of the Flies* in here!" Everyone got the reference and the moniker stuck.

Sometimes after work we would all ride over to the Barton Springs pool in Zilker Park just south of Town Lake and to the west of downtown. The pool at Barton Springs isn't a pool in the typical sense; it's much better. The Edwards aquifer runs underground and springs up to the base of Barton Creek to create a pool two football fields long. The pool has a natural granite bottom, none of that sky-blue concrete, and the water is frigid in August and pleasantly warm in January. It's a great place to go after a day of pushing yourself to near exhaustion. Plus, from April through October, the surrounding bluffs are packed with beautiful women. Reagan, Cliff, Jorge, Zeke and I would wash off and the guys would become squirrels looking for a nut, all except Zeke. He was always with Laura. As I waded in the freezing water listening to a drum circle on the other side of the fence, I realized how glad I was to be here. It was just one of those moments.

5

The Stubb Foundation

Summer 1997

Song on the radio: "Jumper" by Third Eye Blind
Visit <u>www.michaeljuge.com</u> on the *Here We Are Now* page to listen

Logos called me to substitute for a courier who was assigned to one of their other client offices one Tuesday morning. I had spent the first half of the summer hanging out with the Lord of the Flies crew learning the city and getting better at trail riding. They still gave me shit for my pretty mountain bike, but all in all they grew on me. I ended up having them over to my co-op on Fridays while they drank. It was summer, so all the other residents at the Harvest Moon Co-op had left. It was just Stacy and me living there. If the other co-op residents knew what kind of carnivorous Caligula-esque, Bacchanalian debauchery we threw, they would have been forced to set the house on fire. Though a political radical herself, Stacy liked having the boys over. They were fun. She even was okay with Reagan once she cut him down to size the way he needed after he made some lewd offers. And as for me, I had become the crew's token college boy. I guess we bonded in the land of the Lord of the Flies, so I was a little apprehensive when I got the call from headquarters to go to another office.

"What's the place?" I asked skeptically.

"It's the Stubb Foundation," the disembodied voice of middle management said on the phone.

"The barbecue place?"

Okay, let me qualify that for the Austin-impaired. Stubbs is a BBQ restaurant in downtown that has live music, of course.

"Not *Stubbs* . . . It's the Stubb Foundation. It's a . . ." there was a pause. "The Stubb Foundation does something in technology," middle management guy said, cryptically.

I cycled down Barton Springs Road westbound from South 1st Street looking for the appropriate cross street that I had drawn on my map. This was back before smart phones. GPS was still primarily the domain of the military. Back in the day, we had to ask for directions and draw squiggly lines on paper. That's why I always carried a legal pad and a city map to draw my own routes. I had probably passed The Stubb Foundation dozens of times since moving to Austin, and I had never noticed it before now. Hidden behind untended brush was a very unusual two-story building hoisted up perhaps two stories atop concrete columns. Smoke-tinted windows comprised the walls that formed a hexagonal-shaped building with an industrial gray concrete roof and floor. It didn't fit any type of office building design that I had become familiar with. It looked like it might have been a mansion, but it was probably the funkiest-looking mansion I had seen. Judging by the style, I guessed it was perhaps built in the '70s when they envisioned the future with a lot of hard angles and joyless utilitarianism despite the all-encompassing windows. I pedaled off down the side street to the entrance. The building looked to be in disrepair. Weeds sprouted out from the driveway, the chain link gate was crooked and there was spray paint on one of the concrete columns supporting the building. I would have said it was abandoned, but there was a red Saab parked underneath. I noticed a mailbox leaning at an angle next to where I was standing. Thanks to *the X-Files*, I was struck with a momentary flash of investigative ingenuity. I figured if I were Special Agent Fox Mulder, I would check the mailbox to see if this place got any mail and who it went to. The box was full and all of it was addressed to the Stubb Foundation, so I was definitely at the right place. Maybe the company suddenly tanked. It wouldn't be the first time I rode over to a dotcom only to find that all of the office furniture had been removed and the copper stripped from the walls.

The gate was unlocked, so I figured I should at least go in and see if there was anyone home. I parked my bike and walked up the stairs. There was an elevator, but I had this fear that it would break down and I would be stuck inside an elevator in a potentially abandoned building. When I got to the top, I could see that there were people inside. One of them waved me in. I then felt this strange sense of déjà vu. It lasted several seconds until I opened the door. A scrawny young guy greeted me.

"Are you from Logos?" he asked.

"Yes, hi. My name is Chris."

The guy slapped his hands together and gave a thumbs up.

"Thank God!"

Confused, I stuttered, "Um, yeah, no problem. Logos won't leave you hanging."

"No!" he said excitedly. "That you're a Chris. The other Chris was not the Chris we were looking for."

I didn't know how to respond to that. I never figured my parents' lack of imagination in naming me would serve me well.

"Yeah, sure."

The guy introduced himself. "I'm Helmut Spankmeister."

I did everything in my power to maintain a neutral expression and not go into a fit of giggles. Hell, I didn't even know if he was just joking around. *Helmut Spankmeister . . .* It's pronounced exactly how you think it is. I considered the distinct possibility he was screwing with me, but I figured it was better to be a mark than to offend.

"Pleased to meet you, Mr. Spank . . ."

"Call me Helmut!" He looked to be my age, so it would have been weird to use formal titles even if he had a normal last name. "And this here is Sheila."

Helmut looked like he just came down from a tree. He had long, unkempt hair, a scraggly beard and wore a plain white T-shirt with stains and jeans. Sheila didn't hold such a professional appearance. She had dyed platinum blonde hair on top of dyed red roots. She wore these thick glasses, but it wasn't a fashionable thing back then, and *My Little Pony* pajamas.

"Pleased to meet you," I said offering my hand.

Sheila just gave the traditional salutation of a stiff nod.

"Sheila doesn't like to be touched," Helmut explained.

"Oh."

Helmut gave me a quick tour. The Stubb Foundation had an impressive view of the city perched up as it was and walled on all sides by glass. Austin didn't have much of a skyline back then, but you could see Town Lake, the jogging trail and the Clarksville neighborhood on the other side. If this place had been a mansion, I could at least say the previous owner had an eye for location even if the architect had an aversion to anything approaching warm or comforting. Picture a huge living room, a dance hall even. That was the main floor of the Stubb Foundation.

As a bike messenger, most of my deliveries were limited to downtown and the campus area. Most businesses there were law offices, title companies, state government offices and university buildings. The majority of dotcoms tended to situate themselves in the west hills, usually off of the 360. But there were enough in the downtown area for me to be familiar with the basic office culture, "office" being a relative term for dotcoms.

Dotcoms absolutely abhorred anything approaching an "office." They went out of their way to make their employees feel at home. It wasn't unusual to see some guy working on a project sitting on a beanbag outside with a long Ethernet cord connecting his laptop to the World Wide Web. Some dotcoms even had nap rooms—that's right, rooms specifically designed for the purpose of sleeping while at work. I thought that was both neat and completely ridiculous. The Stubb Foundation took it a step further.

"This is where I usually reside," Helmut said. In front of me was a bed with *Jurassic Park* bed sheets. Next to it was a desk that held a jumble of computer equipment. There were a couple of live computer monitors inside the darkened cove beneath the desk in the space where your legs would be if you were sitting like a normal person.

"But we sort of move around as necessary," Helmut added.

There wasn't any particular separation between one person's space and another. It all sort of blended together. Computer monitors and TV screens sat on the floor, some on dining tables, and some were nestled inside shelves while circuit boards were stapled along the interior walls and linked to each other in a tapestry of wire and duct tape. I counted twenty beds in total, leading me to the conclusion that this was a small office, if that was the right term.

An obese guy sitting on an old La-Z-Boy with a faded plaid design typed on his laptop while a mobile black and white TV on static rested in the crook of his arm.

Helmut led me around to the back where there was a clearing for a school desk and chair. Against the surrounding bedlam, the sparse school space looked creepy the way hearing a music box playing a lullaby in a horror movie did.

"Here. Take a seat."

As I sat down, Helmut handed me a Scantron sheet and a little booklet. The cover showed the Stubb Foundation logo, which was the first I saw of it. I didn't see any markings outside the building or even when I walked into the reception area which by the way had no reception desk. Actually, I really couldn't say there was a "reception area," just an entrance and there you were, inside the Stubb Foundation. The logo looked to be a purple blooming flower levitating over the infinity sign, meaning the sideways "8," not the car company.

The Stubb Foundation

Employee Diegetic Analysis and Assessment

"Please take as little time as needed," he said professionally.

I had already taken an aptitude test and was going to mention that, but when I opened the test booklet, I was intrigued by some of the questions. So, I went to it. Some were history questions, some were basic math and then it got weird . . . quick.

-Who was your favorite teacher?
    A. Mr. Martinez
    B. Mrs. Brown
    C. Mrs. White
    D. Mr. Kerry

How in the hell was I supposed to answer this? Had I missed something? Was there some video I was supposed to have watched first before answering this one? Helmut had walked off several minutes ago, and I wasn't sure how urgent it was to pry myself out of the seat to find him and ask. Then something occurred to me. I recognized every name in the list of options. I had a teacher with the name of each of the choices. But then again, those were common enough names. Mrs. Brown was definitely my favorite teacher, so I circled "B" on the Scantron.

There were a few more normal questions, and then it had questions about things like making iced coffee. There was a question about bicycle maintenance. And then there was this odd one.

-What is the fundamental flaw in nihilism?
    A. There's no point to it
    B. Nihilism incorrectly presumes that there is no objective reality
    C. The Subject/object relational duality, though flawed, is dependent upon the other for existence

Finally! Something put my philosophy degree to use.

After I finished up, I found Helmut outside on the balcony talking on a cell phone. He got off, collapsed the antenna and took the Scantron from me. He looked at it and he smiled.

"Perfect," he whispered. "Fantastic!" He hurried inside and met with the other folks at the Stubb Foundation. The sliding doors were closed, so I couldn't hear what they said, but Helmut was gesturing wildly with excitement. It looked like the entire Stubb Foundation gathered around him, possibly twenty or thirty of them. I was tempted to walk inside and see what all the fuss was about, but I figured it was best to stay outside. Apparently, I must have done well, because Helmut pointed to the Scantron and the people applauded.

After a few minutes, Helmut walked outside followed by everyone else and extended his hand.

"Congratulations! I think you might be the Chris."

"'The Chris?' That is freaking odd."

"I know, right?"

Stacy and I were hanging out at Flipnotics Coffeehouse on Barton Springs before our next AA meeting. Flipnotics was my favorite coffeehouse. It wasn't the coffee so much, though the brew was great. I think it had more to do with location. It looked like a surfer shop butted up on the side of a hill. Also, they had a great selection of T-shirts to choose from. Stacy had been out of town for a few days and so I caught her up to speed about my new assignment.

"'The Chris.' That's what he said."

"Who?"

"The guy Helmut."

"His name is Helmut?"

"Yeah, Helmut Spankmeister."

Stacy spat coffee on the table as she struggled to catch her breath from laughing so hard.

"Yeah, I know. It wasn't easy for me to repeat his name with a straight face."

"Is he German?"

"No. I don't think so. He doesn't have an accent or anything. He's really nice, actually. You'd like him."

"Oh, I'm sure."

"Helmut said . . ." she laughed again, so I pressed on over her. "*Helmut* then went on to say that the last Chris wasn't 'Chris enough' and that he was clearly not 'the Chris.' They thought he could be, but it turned out he wasn't."

"What the hell does that mean?"

I shrugged. "Beats me. All I know is that place is truly bizarre. But they seem chill. Also, I think this new assignment might be a windfall for me."

After the Stubb Foundation crew congratulated me, they asked if I had a vehicle and were pleased that I did. Fortunately, Stacy had since bought her own car, a Toyota Camry, which was more reliable than *Value Menus*. Helmut handed me a price sheet showing how they paid for their deliveries. It required a degree in mathematics to figure out but here's what I determined.

- Deliveries between 0-5 miles in a vehicle paid $7 per delivery.
- That same distance paid $11 on bicycle.
- They paid $15 for that same distance on bike if it was raining
- and $17 whenever it was over 98 degrees.
- For deliveries between 5-10 miles they paid $15 per delivery in a vehicle and $11 per bicycle.

At this point I dropped the theory that they were trying to support green transportation. The list just got stranger from there. Fortunately, I didn't have to pay close attention anyway, because I had come home today with a wad of cash for the mileage. That was the other thing: They paid in cash.

"Have you heard of the Stubb Foundation?"

Stacy's brows furrowed. "They sound familiar, actually."

"From work?"

"Hmm, I don't know. I think so. What do they do?"

"Well, that's just it. I'm not exactly sure."

Frankly, I never paid much attention to what the client office did. I didn't really know what kind of law they practiced at my last assignment at Taylor, Swift and Lavigne. I moved documents to and from title companies, medical offices, you name it. They might have done a little of everything.

"I asked Helmut what they did there and he simply said that they are a nonprofit organization committed to saving the universe from annihilation."

"And that doesn't sound odd?"

"Well, I think Helmut was just being cute. Anyway, they have all of this tech stuff all over the place, and they had me deliver documents to all these dotcoms all over town. So, I figured you might know about them."

"Sounds like they're an incubator."

"Hmm. I'm not going to say they wear diapers, but they sure are some strange ass momma's boys and girls."

"No, that's . . . nevermind. I could check at the office tomorrow and see if we have any dealings with them."

"At Rapture?"

"Yeah, of course."

Last month, Stacy had left Alta Vista to work for Rapture. It was hard keeping up with where she was employed.

"What is it y'all do again?"

Stacy sighed. "Okay, when people were programming computers back in the '70s and '80s, they programmed the year with two digits. For instance, instead of using all four digits in '1997,' computers were programmed to only recognize the last two digits '97.' The problem is that in a few years, less than three in fact, it's going to be 2000. So, when 2000 arrives, the date on the computers will cycle back to '00.'"

"Okay, what's wrong with that?" I asked.

"Because, Chris, the computers are going to think it's the year 1900, not 2000."

"Whaaa?"

Stacy went on to explain that programmers back in the day didn't think things through when they did two-digit codes—either that or it was collective laziness on the part of programmers. In the end, it came to haunt the industrialized world. With 2000 approaching, banks, airlines, everyone was freaking out. "Y2K." That's what they called it. Y2K could muck everything up seriously. It could even cause the demise of Western Civilization.

The homies—that's what they called their employees at Rapture—they were all focused on patching operating systems and mainframe computers with four-digit year codes. It sounded like a valiant effort and the more she described Y2K the more it sounded like the failure to adequately patch the systems could cause havoc. Y2K. Didn't want that to happen. Unlike most dotcoms whose mission statements sounded as airy as my resume, Rapture seemed to have a real mission and purpose.

My move to the Stubb Foundation introduced me to the world of dotcoms as my courier work expanded to include deliveries in *Value Menus*. Startups sprouted up all along the west side of Austin during the '90s. They were an entirely different order animal from traditional businesses. Whether the dotcom was a software engineering firm, a game developer, in web design, or in commercial database design, they shared certain qualities. Wherever I went I saw the same elements. Dotcoms were desperate to appear original, pioneering and daring. They wanted to stand out from the fray, and they wanted their employees to think "outside the box."

In pursuit of that, they did all sorts of wacky things. I once dropped in on a company while the employees were playing hide and go seek. It was some kind of team building exercise they told me sheepishly after this FedEx guy and I spent 40 minutes trying to find the R&D department. One time, I went over to Aries 9 off of Bee Caves Road and found the entire IT department doing arts and crafts with construction paper and glue. They also had a hot tub. The Stubb Foundation frequently sent me to The Rancorp on Spicewood Springs Road. Like many dotcom offices, they had hip, Indie music playing on the intercoms. That's great and all, but The Rancorp had its own fulltime DJ in the lobby spinning for the company. I walked in hearing the *dmp dmp dmp* sound of house music and felt as though I should be shuffling through a sweaty throng of people rolling on ecstasy.

Beanbags, napping stations, and ergonomically designed chairs were common. Many places gave their employees cell phones and laptops with no assigned desk. Some companies had fulltime masseuses to give back rubs to anyone on site. Naturally, there was no dress code. I would walk in seeing my Gen X peers either dressed as shabbily as the folks at The Stubb Foundation or completely decked out ready to go clubbing.

There were variations on the theme, but every dotcom was seeking to set itself apart. If they couldn't do it by whatever they were selling, they would at least try to create new environs that were, admittedly, enjoyable places to spend your time. Every dotcom was progressive thinking and every dotcom—every last one of them—had a weekly beer bash on Fridays starting usually around 3 p.m.

When it came to their beer bashes, dotcoms competed with each other to be the dopest, most happening spot in town. They had the best beer on tap, and wait staff with trays of hors d'ouevres. I usually didn't need to worry about dinner if I set my deliveries just right. What was the occasion? It was a Friday. That's all the reason they needed to throw these lavish weekly parties. If I had any deliveries to a dotcom after 3 p.m. and I needed to deliver something to the data administrator personally, I knew to just ask the drunken receptionist where the deck was, because that was where I would find everyone.

My deliveries exposed me to all parts of the city. Some work had me going up to Dell in Round Rock, which bore a striking resemblance to a suburb of Dallas. Actually, I think the entire town of Round Rock is a subsidiary of Dell. The Stubb Foundation also sent me south from time to time to Southwest University in San Marcos. San Marcos is for those who just couldn't handle the urban hustle and bustle of Austin. I couldn't say what Southwest University did other than holding class outside.

I noticed that the bioregional division between the east and west sides of Austin extended itself socio-economically as well. I would occasionally go to the eastside to some industrial park for a delivery, but never once did I find a dotcom located more than a football field's length east of the I-35. All of them were located west of the interstate. There seemed to be this unwritten rule about dotcoms that unless your office was perched precariously over some cliff, it wasn't worth setting up shop there. The only exception to the rule I could find in the high tech circuit was Dell itself and its subsidiary businesses in Round Rock. It was their loss, because the best barbecue in town was east of the city.

I really couldn't say what business the Stubb Foundation had with all of these other businesses, much less what a lot of these other businesses did other than the fact that they were in high tech. I examined some of their posters in the lobbies hoping to get a clue, but most just showed the same print of a gorilla brandishing a thighbone over a horde of other gorillas with the message "Contemporize."

Coffee Part I: Starbucks and the rise of the coffeehouse

In the 1990s, the coffeehouses emerged to become a thing. Certainly, coffeehouses had always been popular gathering spots within artsy corners in select cities, my hometown being one of them, but it wasn't until the '90s that the coffeehouse expanded its reach to the most common subdivision throughout every city in the country. There were a variety of reasons why the coffeehouse boom hit in the '90s as opposed to the '80s or '70s. One reason was the young generation searching for something "authentic." Coffeehouses (before mass Starbuckinization) offered a more intimate environment with unique flavors. You might have noticed the rise of coffeehouses coincided with the rise of microbreweries. It's the same concept. Globalization, increased disposable incomes, and grunge byproducts of the Seattle scene were other factors.

But the most crucial factor is the rise of Starbucks. Some may recall a time before Starbucks, but most of us can't remember what was there before a Starbucks opened shop. Starbucks has that memory erasing effect. I believe there are entire villages that once existed that were erased from the collective memory of man and replaced by a Subway shop and Starbucks.

As much as it pains me to say, I'll say it: Starbucks has its place. I was one of those who railed against them. I called them the "evil empire." But the fact is Starbucks actually inspired more independent coffeehouses to open during the '90s partly in response to the ubiquitous green logo screaming homogenization. Plus, they introduced Middle America to decent coffee. Through Starbucks, regular Americans were gently indoctrinated into and educated in the coffee arts in an environment that didn't intimidate them. As a result, you can go to any backwoods, one-horse town today and know that there has to be at least one place, "even just a Starbucks," to get some decent coffee.

Despite the vitriol I had for them back in the day, I have come to accept them as a legitimate place to get coffee on the condition that there is no local coffeehouse within a 4-mile radius by car, 1 mile by bike (November-May, of course), 1/3 mile by foot (not raining and same cool season weather applies) or ½ mile by bike or 1/8 mile on foot from Mid-May through October. Airport terminal Starbucks is completely kosher.

See my chart on distances to travel for quick reference.

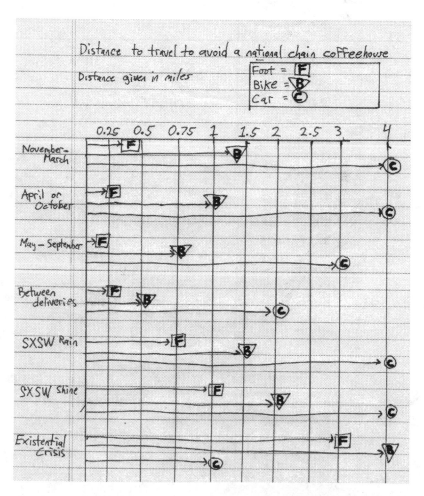

6

Hillary vs. El Guapo

Autumn 1997

I was at Ruta Maya Coffeehouse with Raquel to support her boyfriend Ejay who had been signed to play tonight. I really liked Ejay. He was genuine and friendly, one of those real sensitive types. In fact, he was Mr. Sensitive Ponytail guy, except he didn't have a ponytail being half African-American and all. He played a lot of Joni Mitchell and Bob Denver covers. Politely, I applauded. He had a nice voice and sang from the heart, though I have to say it did make me squirm a bit.

After the show, Ejay gave me a hug hello and kissed Raquel.

"Hello, my love," he said.

"Sweetie, loved your rendition of 'Just the way you are.'"

"Ah, thanks!"

"All right, you two." I broke the love fest up. I wasn't jealous really, just a little perturbed. "Hey, I'm meeting Stacy tonight for this thing. You guys want to join me?"

"What kind of thing?"

"It's a robot fighting match or something."

Ejay stroked his goatee. "Hmm. Sounds kind of violent. Besides, I wanted to take Raquel to Dobie. They're showing *Like Water for Chocolate* in 3-D."

"Wow, 3-D, huh? Sounds like a blockbuster night. Well, you two have fun."

We conversed a little while longer and the discussion invariably wound its way to this new show *South Park* on Comedy Central. It was all the rage. When it was time to head out, I walked next door to The Ginger Man to find Reagan and Cliff picking up on some college girls.

"Chris, are we going or what? I am totally wasted and I want to get my fight on!"

Song getting a lot of airplay:
"Mo Money Mo Problems" by The Notorious B.I.G.
Visit www.michaeljuge.com on the *Here We Are Now* page to listen

Usually when you think of robot death matches, you think of . . . well, you don't think about farms. That's where this robot match was taking place. It was way the hell southeast on the 183 well deep into El Chupacabra territory. I thought I had passed it or gotten the directions wrong until I saw the turn off and a horde of vehicles parked outside a barn. The owner of the barn rented it out for a variety of events: weddings, square dancing, robot death matches . . . I waded through the crowd searching for Stacy.

"Chris!" Stacy waved until I spotted her.

"Hey, I'd like you to meet my friend Tara. She's entering the fight tonight. Tara, this is Chris."

Tara wore a flowing earth tone dress and sandals and had this cute black pixie hairstyle going.

"So . . . you're 'the Chris,' eh?" Apparently, Stacy had told Tara about the Stubb Foundation's moniker for me.

"I am he," I replied.

We talked while I drank my iced coffee from my big blue plastic cup that I always brought to social events like beer bashes, birthday parties and even robot death matches. I noticed that I do quite well socializing when I'm wired.

"So, who's this?" I asked gesturing to the menacing-looking toolbox with a circular saw.

"Let me introduce you to Hillary. She don't flex nuts, because she doesn't have to," Tara said confidently interlacing hip hop lingo with her refined speech. "Besides, she doesn't have any."

As far as gladiator robots went, Hillary was not much to look at. Its chassis, like the other contestants, had a low center of gravity. The circular saw on its arm looked like it could do some real harm to a human, but it remained to be seen how effective it would be on reinforced armor.

An announcer on a bullhorn pulled up to the center of the barn. The ring was cordoned off by flimsy panels that Hillary's saw could probably tear through without slowing down, but it served to keep the spectators and controllers away from the ring.

"Yo, biatches, let's do this!" the announcer called with a roar of approval.

He introduced the first fight of the evening and money started exchanging hands. A kid at the chalkboard took bets 'til the air horn squealed to begin the fight. This was definitely not a sanctioned event by the State of Texas. I just hoped the cops wouldn't show up. The first match pitted a racecar blender against a fire-breathing tank. The fire did nothing to the blender, though it delighted the audience. It also set one of the panels of the ring on fire, but they had a fire extinguisher handy— this probably wasn't the first fire-breathing robot they encountered. The blender attacked ferociously, yet it was bested by the tank, which crawled on top of it. The tank had a secret weapon—hydraulics, and proceeded to hump the blender to death. I never thought I would ever see that.

Next up was a modified vacuum cleaner against what looked like NASA's Pathfinder, which had just landed on Mars a few weeks ago. It was a draw. Tara was a picture of concentration as she made finishing touches to Hillary, placing a blonde wig on the toolbox-shaped robot.

The announcer cleared his throat. "All right, playas, next up, we got a treat for you. We got last year's champion back. Directly from San Jose, California"—there was a chorus of boos—"the master of disaster, the mack daddy of Silicon Valley, I give you . . . El Guapo!" From the opposite side of the barn rolled a massive looking toaster on treads with two hammer arms. It was followed by the controller, a really obese dude wearing a Gwar T-shirt and his minion holding a ghetto blaster playing "Mama said knock you out" by LL Cool J.

Tara took a deep cleansing breath.

"Facing El Guapo, coming straight from the south side of Austin—she's a real ball buster, yo, so you better give some room. I present . . . Hillary!"

Hillary had her own theme song, too. It was L7's "Shitlist." Tara had me hold the ghetto blaster while she used the remote to guide Hillary to the ring. The audience gave muted applause for the little blonde robot. At first I thought my perspective was off, but it wasn't. El Guapo was massive. It dwarfed little Hillary, the little circular saw-wielding toolbox. The announcer was also the referee and set the rules:

- Don't do anything to the controller
- No human interference inside the ring
- When the air horn is blown, cease action
- There was a final reminder of Asimov's laws of robotics to ensure that everyone knew that operators were strictly forbidden to do anything unethical like allowing the robot to go on a killing spree.

Tara gave a terse nod to the referee, a head nod to the opponent and they went to their corners. The referee blew the air horn and the fight was on. El Guapo went directly on the attack, approaching Hillary and smashing its hammer arms. But Hillary was fast. That little toolbox got out of the way just in time. So, she—I mean, *it* survived the first crucial seconds. El Guapo lumbered giving chase while Hillary had surprising maneuverability on its side. Hillary made its first attack with the saw but hit nothing vital on El Guapo's frame. Then Hillary ran back. El Guapo then smashed back, but didn't make contact.

All the while I was looking at Tara on the controls. Her pixie black hair and tattoo of a Cheshire cat on her arm became all the more attractive as this lady fought the monster. The match continued for several minutes with no one getting the edge on the other. El Guapo was too massive to take head on while Hillary was too agile and quick to pin down. The audience was getting impatient.

I heard Reagan yelling, "We want blood!" He was drunk off his ass but he voiced the precise sentiment of the crowd. People started booing at the stalemate.

Suddenly, El Guapo seized up. The controller was working frantically on the remote control, but nothing. El Guapo smashed it hammers on the ground in a fit, but Hillary was nowhere near the business end. Tara moved swiftly and took advantage of the situation. Hillary extended its circular saw and moved towards El Guapo's arms. It was messy, there was a horrible screeching sound as the saw cut through the metal, but Hillary managed to cut off El Guapo's arms, its hammers fell lifelessly to the ground. The crowd cheered. El Guapo's controller was finally able to get El Guapo to move back ever so slowly, but then it died again.

The crowd started chanting. I couldn't make it out at first, but soon enough everyone including myself joined in. "Two bots enter, one bot leaves! Two bots enter, one bot leaves!"

Tara knew what she had to do. Encouraged, she guided Hillary around to face El Guapo, whose brain was now exposed without its arms to protect it. Hillary spun the saw and cut into El Guapo. The robot started to shake and smoke. The audience roared in delight. Tara turned around and kissed me on the cheek.

As you can guess, after seeing such a display, I was kind of smitten with Tara. It wasn't just the fact that she, through her avatar, had laid a smack down on a hammer-pounding turtle machine, though that would warm the cockles of any man's heart. It was more. She was so . . . spirited, spritely. I made a point to make the beer bashes at Rapture not to hang with Stacy so much as to see Tara. She always wore those flowing dresses and was so optimistic and happy about life. She could turn the most grizzled curmudgeon by her mere presence. So, one afternoon, we were all hanging out on the deck overlooking the hills. Stacy was chatting up one of the guys there when I saw Tara. I had finished my deliveries for the day. My last one was to a Dell venture company that was developing a way to record onto DVD. I thought that would be great if I could one day put all of my VHS tapes onto something much more portable. I drank the rest of my iced coffee to get my liquid courage and made my way over to Tara.

I was funny, I was charming, and it was a sunny autumn day in Austin meaning it was in the low 70s. Life was good. So, I did my line.

"So, Tara, I was wondering if you would like to . . . you know . . . meet,"

"I'm gonna stop you right there, tiger," she interrupted. "I'm gay."

Damn. "Oh . . . well, then. Um, wow."

"That's not a problem for you, is it?" she asked suspiciously.

"Oh that? No, not at all. Hell, Stacy and I are the token breeders at our place. No, I'm good with that. But I guess it would make it impractical to continue to ask you out."

"Sorry, big guy," she said as she softly hit my arm.

I was a little embarrassed at first, but I consoled myself in the fact that there was nothing to be done about it. I was the wrong sex for her. End of story. That evening, I came home and I felt really alone as I watched the episode on *The X-Files* that took place in the recent past back in 1990 where Mulder was introduced to the Lone Gunmen at an electronics expo. Stacy spent a lot of her time with a boyfriend and getting involved with the Greens. I felt like a third wheel with Zeke and his girlfriend sometimes, and I just didn't want to be divested of my hard-earned money this week joining Reagan and Cliff trolling gentlemen's clubs and karaoke bars.

I hopped on my Kona and cycled off from the Harvest Moon Co-op. The weather had finally broken into pleasantly cool evenings, making the ride west along Enfield enjoyable. I thought about things. It was when I cycled that I processed a lot of thoughts that had been stirring just below the surface.

How long will I be working in this job? Will I ever figure out what I'm supposed to do with my life? Dude, shouldn't you call your sponsor? Aidan gets really pissed when you don't call. How would things have turned out had I not gotten sober? What if I never left New Orleans? Would that Venetian cream induced-vision I had have come true? Could it still?

I cycled all the way up to Mount Bonnell. The sun had set and the sky turned violet as I carried my bike up the steps to the summit. At the top of the staircase stood a historical marker next to a low-set limestone wall that served as the only barrier before the precipice. Hundreds of feet below churned Lake Austin. I could see the rust-colored bridge of the 360 Highway where most of the dotcoms were settled. Just below along Lake Austin were the villas of all the Dellionaires, folks who invested in Dell back in the day when it was little more than a few guys making computers inside an apartment. I walked along the dusty precipice arguing with myself. I made the case that I really shouldn't get so down about being rejected by a lesbian. But it wasn't Tara at all, really. I had been in a funk for days. I stood on the precipice positioning myself in my signature regal stance overlooking the Hill Country. If this were a movie, I thought to myself, there would be a great moment where the main character had an epiphany. Unfortunately, I cycled home with a clichéd movie scene but no epiphany.

7

78704: It's not just a zip code.
It's a way of life

1998

Monologue committed to memory: the details of Dr. Evil's life

I managed to get kicked out of the Harvest Moon Co-op. Normal
places you get kicked out for drugs, stealing, assault or some other crime
of moral turpitude. In my case it was nothing so juicy. I didn't steal, I
didn't cause any disturbance. I didn't piss in the communal lemonade.
Don't ask why I came up with that scenario. And drugs? First of all, I'm
sober, so that didn't happen, and second, so long as it was pot, 'shrooms,
acid or ecstasy, the housemates encouraged drug use. So, what was my
crime? "Repeated carnivory in a vegan household." I had been caught
eating meat, consuming the flesh of animals inside the sacred grounds
of Harvest Moon Co-op. Stacy warned me. She told me to be careful
about my culinary choices. Stacy successfully managed to live in a vegan
household for three years.

But during the summer while all the wet blankets were at home
enraging their parents, Stacy and I had a Lollapalooza of cookouts laden
with meat. When school started again, we had to button up our ways.
I guess I got lazy. One morning they found Taco Cabana wrappers in
my room, the smoking gun. There was a Commission on Truth and
Reconciliation—that's what they called it, and I freely admitted to

eating meat inside the house; furthermore, I volunteered that I had been bringing in fried chicken almost every night for a year now. And that was it. I was out. Me and my decadent ways were voted off the Utopian island of Harvest Moon Co-op. This was before *Survivor,* so there were no copyright infringements.

Maybe I wanted out. I had been making a good living over at Logos assigned to the Stubb Foundation as I was. It wasn't like the desperate early months at Terminal Car Rentals where I could barely make rent. I was getting *paid.* Those crazy bastards at the Stubb Foundation didn't seem to have the concept of money nor mileage, and I'll admit it: I took advantage of their cluelessness. But at least that meant I was able to replace an alternator on *Value Menus* without having to freak out about it. I was doing all right, really. So, I didn't need to stay at the co-op any longer. Besides, I was getting tired of sneaking food into my room like a criminal. The more I thought about it, the happier I was.

I was hanging in the copy room at the Law Office of Taylor, Swift and Lavigne. I didn't have any deliveries over there but I had to get out of the Stubb Foundation and talk to some normal people. I always thought working at a dotcom would be fun, but being a Luddite around a bunch of social misfit computer geeks was more isolating than anything. The Stubb Foundation guys weren't like the other dotcom folks I met. Your garden-variety techies in Austin typically were punks like Stacy. Some were hipster types like in *Swingers.* By and large, you could engage in conversation with them. The Stubb Foundation folks were just off. So, I was left to converse with Zeke and the rest of the Lord of the Flies crew spending my social life inside a copy room while fax machines repeated error messages.

"So, your stomach got you in trouble. That's what you're telling me, *cabron?*"

I nodded. He put his hand on my shoulder. "Well, you're in luck, ese. I just so happen to be in need of a couple of roommates myself."

The house on Travis Heights was like a dream. You know those TV shows where these twenty-somethings live in an awesome loft in New York City, and they work at a coffeehouse or are unemployed half-heartedly searching for a job, and you yell at the TV, "That's bullshit!

You couldn't afford that! Nobody could!" That's what I thought about this place. The Travis Heights house was located on Travis Heights Boulevard itself at the crest of a hill. Just south of Town Lake, the Travis Heights neighborhood is sandwiched between South Congress and I-35. Even back in the '90s it was a highly desirable place to live. Today? Forget about it. You couldn't rent a storage shed there.

The house wasn't much to look at from the street. The stone and mortar mid-century looked like a smallish two-bed, one-bath beginner home. That's because the house was built at the top of the hill. But once inside there were stairs leading down to another room and then further down to another, which had a door that led to the back yard. The back yard had a descending series of wooden decks. The yard tumbled down the hill where trash had collected over years. From what Zeke told me, nobody has ever gone to the end of the yard. He didn't know what I would find there. As I walked outside, I looked up and saw that Zeke and Laura's room was the penthouse. Their room extended out into the open with a balcony supported by four wooden beams.

I couldn't believe Zeke and Laura found this place. It was to my great fortune that I got kicked out of the Harvest Moon Co-op, because I left the Egypt of campus area in North Austin for the promised land of South Austin. I landed in the house that I would dream about for years to come, the house where I would fall in love. I would always dream of one day returning to buy this house. I moved into the room furthest downstairs which opened onto the back yard. That evening I ate a bucket of fried chicken openly in the living room with Zeke, Laura and Cliff, who practically lived there anyway, while I introduced them to the *X-Files*. I felt liberated eating greasy chicken in public. When I told Stacy about another empty room at the house, she quickly ate a plate of ribs at the Harvest Moon Co-op in front of everyone and joined me.

8

The multiple choice existential crisis

Spring 1998

Song played at the HEB grocery store:
"I Got Shit" by Pearl Jam
Visit **www.michaeljuge.com** on the *Here We Are Now* page to listen

I had been working at the Stubb Foundation for a few months, so I had gotten used to their quirks. They ordered Mexican food every day promptly at 10:30, usually from Chuys. Any deviation from this routine was rare. Helmut had the Elvis Presley Memorial combo, Stella the Chuychanga, Sheila the combo plate #3, and so on. Once in a blue moon I could get them to agree on Jovitas or El Mercado, but they spent hours doing the calculus of what would provide the same exact experience they got from Chuys. Like the vast majority of restaurants, Chuys didn't have its own website yet, so the Stubb Foundation created one for them, volunteering to be their service provider for free. You know how you order food online without thinking about it? That's the Stubb Foundation. Chuys naturally accepted their kind offer and the Stubb Foundation got free T-shirts in return.

On Fridays, I would run over to HEB grocery store on Oltforf and stock the massive freezer with Hot Pockets to last them over the weekend. I sorted through their mail. There was a lot of misdirected mail that was meant for Stubbs BBQ. The Stubb Foundation didn't have a receptionist or any other employees outside the little cabal other than myself. I did my bike-mounted deliveries downtown to rake up the cash, especially when it rained (see the chart). I did my pickup truck deliveries throughout the greater metro area and they let me schedule them in the way that was most convenient for me. For instance, I would do my deliveries to iSoar whenever I wanted a latte. Stacy said iSoar was some joint venture between Tivoli and Motorola. Whatever. All I knew was that iSoar had a great espresso bar, and I was interested in the barista. They even let me go mountain biking in the Greenbelt on particularly slow days. They gave me my own space where I replaced the school desk. I added some beanbags and Helmut remarked that my corner looked like a cat's cradle. I also liked how they would call me "the Chris." They pretty much gave me free reign.

So, I had no reason to complain when I walked in one morning and Helmut handed me another Scantron and test booklet. I was slightly jarred by this. It reminded me that I was still an outsider, a contract courier from Logos Office Solutions and not one of them. I was about to get into a funk about being a college-educated bike messenger when Helmut reminded me that there was a time limit. He seemed oblivious to the slight I felt, so I just sat down on the school desk, which I swore I had thrown out.

The booklet had the official Stubb Foundation logo like the initial test. The Stubb Foundation did, in fact, have the logo on the building contrary to what I had initially thought. I located it after working there a couple of weeks. It's not obvious. Instead of having their logo inscribed on a marble marker, they spray-painted it onto one of the concrete pillars supporting the building. In essence they tagged their logo with all the propriety of, say, the Crips rather than hiring a designer to craft a proper sign.

The first couple of questions were typical test questions. What's the square of a hypotenuse, who was president of the United States on August 6, 1945? What happened on that date? I know my history. Math? *Meh.* There were some philosophical and theological questions like:

–Origen of Alexandria is famous for what statement?
    A. "What hath Athens to do with Jerusalem?"
    B. "Ain't no thang but a chicken wang."
    C. "Conscience is the chamber of justice."

I answered "C."

–In a pre-deterministic universe
    A. Time is irrelevant as it is an illusion to the objects in play.
    B. Time is immutable
    C. Time and space interact in a fluid still contained within a conscious narrative
    D. We still have free will even if the choices have already been made.

That was a hard one. I settled on B as it was probably the least likely to be refuted, which is not to say it was the most accurate answer.

–Can there be a pre-destination paradox?
    A. Yes, because time does not move in a strictly linear path.
    B. No, because that would require nonlinear movement of time, i.e. time travel into the past, and Einstein proved that to be impossible.
    C. No, because though one can travel back into the past, whatever changes are made create a new reality which is commonly referred to as a "parallel universe" and the time traveler would move in that tangent time stream.
    D. Yes, as evidenced by the advent of solid state electronics in the mid-20th century.

I chose "A."

I figured these questions were not particularly relevant to my job as a courier; however, these very questions had kept me up nights, especially after I was about a year sober or so. But if those questions weren't bizarre enough . . .

–What is the first line you think of when you hear the movie title *Silence of the Lambs*?
    A. "You fly back to school. Fly, fly, fly . . ."
    B. "It places the lotion in the basket."

> C. "I'd fuck me. I'd fuck me hard."
> D. "Ahh!"

"C," definitely "C."

-If you were in the movie *Alive*, but the cast was from the TV show *Alice*, who would you choose to devour?

I won't bother telling you the choices and who I chose. And then the test got more intimate and disturbingly autobiographical.

-Mrs. Brown was your favorite teacher because
> A. She was the first teacher who made me enjoy reading.
> B. She was understanding and helped me learn math.
> C. She gave me a B even though my grades weren't there.
> D. She let us watch cartoons instead of teaching.

This was a follow up question from the first test I took months ago. I had chosen Mrs. Brown, my fourth grade teacher because of answer "A." But how in the hell did they know that? I never told Helmut or anyone else in Austin about something as obscure as about my fourth grade teacher. I filled in the answer, but I was getting a little concerned.

-When did you get sober?
> A. 1995
> B. On December 11th
> C. On a Sunday
> D. I'm drunk at this moment

I wasn't secretive about my sobriety. I might have told one of the Stubb Foundation people about it at some point. I guess if I told them, I also mentioned I got sober on December 11th. It's a little personal, but I'm fine with that. And then came these two.

-What is you most existential fear at this moment?
> A. Roaches

  B. AIDS
  C. That I will be forgotten
  D. That I will never live up to my potential

–What concerns you the most about your future?
  A. How much money I will make.
  B. Creating the best investment portfolio.
  C. Finding the right job.
  D. That I will wander aimlessly from one job to another, never finding what I was meant to do.

I looked around the room. Was I being taped? Was this some sort sick of joke? How in the hell did they know this? Was I that obvious? Or, worse, was I so run-of-the-mill that some of the most existential questions hounding me of late were mundane enough to be included in a standardized test? Both answers were "D," by the way. I handed Helmut the Scantron and went about my deliveries completely befuddled. I couldn't figure how they knew what they knew, nor why my answers mattered to them. A lot of these dotcoms had odd directives that had little to do with their stated mission. For instance, Tara and the entire robotics team were taking swing dancing classes during work hours. Stacy had to lie about her smoking because Rapture just wouldn't allow it. But I bet none of them had to answer whether they would warn President Franklin Roosevelt about Pearl Harbor not knowing the potential consequences in creating alternate timelines or what type of meat most closely resembled human flesh.

  I didn't mind the odd questions so much. It was those last two personal ones that got to me. This was the last thing I needed to be thinking about right now. I had been night cycling a lot lately trying to piece a life plan together. Why did I get sober and others didn't? What did it all mean? How could I make it count? I came up with nothing. Sometimes I rode and the thoughts from the vision would appear. I would cycle harder just trying to get away from the vision.

9

Ah, the smell of a raging Mexican forest fire

Summer 1998

Mexico had a raging forest fire that summer introducing smog to the once-pristine city of Austin. I often heard Reagan chiding Zeke saying that since they couldn't beat us outright, the Mexicans were trying to smoke us out. His response involved the words "chinga" and "pendejo." I wasn't quite sure what those words meant, but I started using them myself in the copy room. Barton Creek had dried up for the summer. I hadn't known an entire body of water could just disappear like that and the event not be considered an ecological disaster. Back in New Orleans there's a puddle in front of my mom's house that has been there since 1983.

Just as there was a change in seasons from spring hot as shit to the summertime you got to be effing kidding me heat, so too, our Travis Heights home had undergone some changes. Zeke and Laura decided to move out so that they could have their own little love nest without me or Stacy interrupting them. I think it might have been my fault. One morning, Zeke, Laura and I were in the kitchen. I was making my iced coffee and prepared to go outside for a smoke. Zeke asked, "You have fun last night?" referring to a date with a really cute girl in IT whom I managed to impress with my friend-making abilities. I might as well be her hairdresser now.

Zeke knew that about me, so maybe I was a little snarky when I responded, "Sounds like you two had a lot more fun than I did."

Zeke gave me one of those, *Dude, what the hell?* looks while Laura buried her shame by cracking the ice tray and dumping the cubes into the bin violently. Laura was a good Catholic girl. She dragged Zeke to church every Sunday. Living in sin and engaging in pre-marital intercourse was probably something Laura had some conflict with. Sure, she felt shame now, but you should have heard them the night before. After they finished, *I* needed a smoke.

Well, I guess I sort of put my foot in it. But instead of kicking me out, Laura decided that it was time for the two of them find themselves a quaint little gated community where they could have the privacy expected for a couple.

Stacy smacked me upside the head. "Way to blow, Chris. Way to blow! Now what in the hell are we gonna do?"

We were both crouching outside in the carport having a smoke. Since she couldn't smoke at work, Stacy made a point to double up on her smoking at home. I was only too happy to oblige. Zeke and Laura had a strict no smoking indoors policy. I had no problem with that. Living at the bottom floor, I just went out to the deck to smoke. Even though they had left, Stacy and I agreed to maintain that policy.

"Well?" she asked. "We were already one roommate short." There was that small room between the ground level and the basement level where I was staying. "And now we're really under water."

"Don't worry, Stacy," I said all confidently. "I have an angle."

"And what angle is that?" she asked.

Okay. I didn't have an angle. But I was one lucky bastard. Before Zeke and Laura moved out, providence handed me not one but *two* roommates! These weren't just any pod knockers you find in the classifieds either (see: *How people did things pre-Craigslist*). No, these were people I already knew. Friends.

Ejay had already expressed interest in taking the nether room tucked between the ground floor and the basement. You remember Ejay, the really kind, sensitive guy dating Raquel, multi-racial dude playing inoffensive acoustic music who worked at Ruta Maya? Yeah, that one. Ejay and I had gotten to know each other over the past several months and hung out independently of Raquel. He was sort of my last line of a positive male role model compatriot, keeping me sane in a world of randy bike messengers pushing me to the dark side. Ejay and I shared an appreciation for Roger Waters and he made me look stolid and reserved in comparison. Well . . . he sort of changed.

Let me explain. Ejay was really in love with Raquel. Whenever he played Hootie and the Blowfish songs, he bore his gaze at her with frightening intensity. I saw the smile she plastered on her face as he sang it. I knew that look because I got it enough myself, though I had the good excuse of being a practicing alcoholic when I held the ghetto blaster playing "In Your Eyes" over my head. When Raquel finished her Masters in Middle Eastern Studies, instead of doing what most people with an MA in Middle Eastern Studies did—go for a PhD in Middle Eastern Studies, I suppose—she decided to join the Israeli Defense Forces. She broke up with Ejay a couple of months before she left. I think Ejay would have been okay with her leaving him to defend the Jewish homeland if it was like *right* before she left, not months in between. There was no clear "I'm leaving you for the future of Israel." So, Ejay withdrew into his economy apartment. I called, but to no avail.

A month later, he emerged from his cocoon. Ejay had transformed into . . . did you see *Gremlins*? He became a player, or as the kids referred to it, a "playa." He quit Ruta Maya to tend bar at Club Deville and became the lead singer of a Ska hop band called Fist Dive. He drank. He womanized. You get the picture. Don't get me wrong. Ejay was still a great guy. Around me, he was still that sensitive young man who played "Killing me softly" with such sincerity. But he was more machine now than man.

I took dibs on Zeke and Laura's room, the awesome master bedroom on the ground floor that extended out to the back complete with the balcony that precariously hung over the tumbling cliff that was our back yard. I didn't realize it until I moved in, but the room was surrounded by windows on three sides like a peninsula. I could smoke freely on the balcony while perched up high with the trees. Someone would one day call it my tree house.

Stacy was fine to stay where she was. She had a fear of heights, so when I brought up doing rock paper scissors for the room, she offered to let me have it in exchange for paying a little extra in rent, and in an ironic gesture, to pay for the Internet access. I still had yet to use a computer despite the fact that Stacy had set up a brand new PC complete with Windows 98 courtesy of her employers at Rapture. Boy, she couldn't get enough of it. She went on and on about how this computer had a one-gigabyte hard drive, 32-megabyte RAM Pentium III processor, CD-ROM, and it also came with a zip drive. I didn't know what any of this meant. She held up this thing that looked like an Atari cartridge.

"You see this, Chris? This is a zip disk. It can hold up to 100 megabytes."

"100 megabytes of what?" I asked innocently. I gave her a look a dog would when a master tried to teach him something in human language.

"Of information!" she yelled. Don't judge her. She had been very patient with me for years, and I had managed to skip the better part of what was being called the Information Revolution not having so much as an email account.

"It can store graphic imagery like when I do web design."

"Wait. I thought you were now working on that Y2K thing."

"I am."

I wanted to confront her on some kind of inconsistency but I couldn't conjure an articulate thought on the subject.

"Okay, well, sure, I'll pay for the service."

Stacy was happy to see Ejay move in. Though she got along with Reagan, Cliff and the other extras from Lord of the Flies, the idea of living under the same roof as them would be a bridge too far. Ejay, despite his newfound lady's man thing, was politically solvent: multi-racial, in a ska hop band, trashed the rest of the state for its regressive policies. Ejay took the basement level that led to the back yard.

And then I found our roommate for the nether room, the room between the ground floor and basement. Tara was a lady of few needs. She didn't own a TV. Her earth tone dresses folded easily into compact Rubbermaid storage containers. She had a modest collection of CDs, all meditation, female artists and world music. So, when I offered the nether room for a discounted price, Tara jumped on it. You might remember Tara from such adventures as the robot war at the barn outside of Lockhart. She kept Hillary oiled up over at her new employer's, Exozert, a third-round startup and soon to be a subsidiary of HP. Exozert was now Hillary's official sponsor. Oh, and Tara also dated Raquel right before she left for Israel.

So, the circle was complete. The Travis Heights house was now fully occupied by Stacy and Raquel's prior conquests.

10

Tis nothing but a G thang

Summer 1998

**Song often heard in the background at parties:
"In The Meantime" by Spacehog**
Visit www.michaeljuge.com on the *Here We Are Now* page to listen

Ejay made a point that we had to make the most of the Travis Heights house. Who could argue? We lived in a house way above our means, and yet here we were. It would be criminal not to take advantage of the place. The parties at our house were kind of weird. When Ejay wasn't doing a show with Fist Dive or working at Club Deville, he was spending his time setting the house up for a party. He would bring his coworkers, band members and lady entourage over. Tara brought over an assorted collection of robotics engineers, IT administrators and graphic designers, while Stacy, though also in the dotcom world, surrounded herself with friends in the Greens, which included at least one obligatory aging hippie. Me? I brought Zeke, Reagan and the rest of the bike messenger guys from Logos.

It was an odd gathering. People like this normally wouldn't hang out. Fortunately, the Lord of the Flies crew mellowed from their more obnoxious behavior when interacting with normal people. And the Greens weren't stereotypical leftist tightwads as I thought they might be. That was more for the International Socialists. The Greens in Austin were dedicated, decidedly left of liberal, but they loved *South Park* like every other Gen Xer and ate barbecue even if it was made out of nut loaf. The tech guys and gals who Tara brought over weren't insular like the Stubb Foundation. They were as outgoing as anyone else. Ejay brought a lot of ladies over. Some of them even talked to me.

The parties had a pattern to them. Ejay would get some of the best appetizers from Central Market sent over a little too early. By the time people started arriving, the cheese started to smell. The main event was outside on the multi-level deck in the tumbling hill of a back yard. Tara hooked up some awesome speakers to this sound system that was not commercially available. It was some prototype that was originally designed for use by the military. For what purpose? I don't know, but the sound system was better than anything I experienced at a movie theater. That was the good news. The bad news was she always wanted to DJ and contended with Ejay for the job. Stacy and I were the only two sober people there so we kept what little order there was. I always had my big blue cup filled with iced coffee. She sometimes had a non-alcoholic beer.

Stacy and the Greens would hang with the Lord of the Flies gang. I always got nervous as hell that a fight would break out. I expected it would, but it never materialized. Still, though, they got me nervous, so I hung out with Ejay where he introduced me to some of his lady friends. Ejay would talk me up, but I found myself talking me into comic relief guy rather than potential hook up.

Tara would play Melissa Etheridge, Lucinda Williams, or PJ Harvey. She was in an estrogen rock phase. I don't know if the Mexican forest fires had anything to do with it. Stacy and Ejay would add their flair, playing anything from the more mainstream Mighty Mighty Bosstones or Soundgarden to the more obscure like Yo La Tengo or Dinosaur Jr. Zeke was still a regular part of the house, so he had to put on 2pac. God, he never would shut up about the "mysterious circumstances" of his death, like it was the Kennedy assassination. "What?" I said, "2pac was a cocky SOB in a macho profession and he pissed off one too many people." This is my issue with Gangsta rap beyond the misogyny and materialism: I just don't like anything that makes country music seem complex and profound in comparison. This was a bone of contention between us, so we agreed to disagree.

I was more into early Pink Floyd, Syd Barrett Pink Floyd. Looking back, I admit it's not particularly good house music. But it's better than back in high school when I listened to Roger Waters and Morrissey exclusively. Talk about eat your own gun. My time as a bass player in Senator Monkey and the Funkicrats didn't open me much to new forms of music.

I overheard certain references at the party from the tech folks, but it wasn't tech jargon. They were discussing money. I should have paid more attention to them. It sounded odd seeing a bunch of youngsters my age with long hair and bowling shirts and wife beaters complete with wallets chained to their pants discussing initial public offerings, stock options and buyouts. They looked normal, but they sounded more like the stuffy business types. I didn't understand most of what they were saying—again, it's my own fault for not reading up on these things. This is what I gleaned from the conversations: This new economy was going to change everything. It would change the laws of physics, by God.

At some point, Ejay, Tara and I would find each other and we would invariably start talking about Raquel. We had each dated her at one time or another and were each dumped by her. Last we heard, Raquel had finished boot camp in the Israeli Defense Forces and was now being trained to become a sniper. Ejay said she was a natural for the job. She had the patience to be still, wait until the moment was right and make the bastard regret ever exposing himself to the world. There's nothing to read into that.

As the night wore on, with Ejay and Tara increasingly intoxicated and me increasingly wired, we would start weaving these intentionally absurd tall tales about Raquel.

"They say that she once built a cabin by herself so that she could nurse an otter back to health."

"One time Raquel slept with my wife, and she made me watch the whole time. It was the most touching thing I've ever seen!"

"Her liver contains a rare element that powers the International Space Station."

Stacy would come over and say something about, "Raquel's rejects," her pet name for us. People got drunker, and between 1 and 2 a.m., they would leave the safety of the decks to wander into the uncharted reaches of the back yard. Things would tumble down the hill; people would tumble down the hill. The next morning, I would find a collection of debris and one or two people accumulated at the base of the yard stopped only by a deteriorating chain link fence. Good times.

Our parties, though odd in other parts of the country, were standard fare here. Austin was eclectic like that. It sort of took the idea of "Let's put these people together from varying demographics, throw in some Tex Mex and gangsta hip hop, and see what happens." Sometimes, we would run over to one of the gated communities, usually the one where Reagan was staying, and would clean ourselves off in the hot tub. Sometimes, we would skinny dip in one of the area pools (I won't say which one).

This one time, Zeke won a most random prize at a school fair raffle whereby he had the use of a limousine and driver for an entire evening in San Antonio. He was about to throw the winning ticket away when Ejay screamed, "Wait! I got an idea!" He grabbed Stacy and put her on the computer. "You're good at doing graphics, right?"

"Yeah, sure."

"Great! Chris, does the Stubb Foundation have a laminating machine?"

"Yeah. They like to laminate things for some reason. Don't ask me why. But what . . ."

"Okay, you bring it here."

Ejay was onto something big. I didn't know what it was but I wanted to be in on it, so I hopped to it and drove over to the Stubb Foundation. I asked Helmut if I could borrow the laminating machine, and he said "of course," but to be sure to return in within 70 hours. I learned not to bother asking why 70 hours and not, say, 72 hours. I brought it home and Ejay and Stacy went to work.

A few days later, the crew of the Travis Heights house along with some of Ejay's band mates arrived in San Antonio and we jumped into the waiting limo Zeke had won for the evening. Ejay handed us laminated IDs on lanyards and gave me an expensive camera to carry. Apparently Stacy, Zeke, and I worked for Details magazine, at least according to the IDs that Ejay and Stacy had forged. We were doing a story on the San Antonio nightlife with one of the former band members of Spin Doctors (i.e., Ejay) who was with his new band. Ejay hoped this charade would not only get us into bars free of cover charges but it would also get us free drinks all night, meaning free Cokes for me and Stacy.

"Um, Ejay . . . I don't know, man. We could get caught."

Ejay gave me one of those soothing shoulder rubs he probably used to seduce women and purred, "Relax, Chris, it's going to be fun."

Ejay was right. Not only did we get into every bar without a cover charge and everyone had free drinks all evening, we were treated like celebrities. People had long forgotten about Spin Doctors and nobody knew what the band members looked like. Fortunately, this was long before people could instantly verify things like Spin Doctors' biographies through Wikipedia on their cell phones. Details magazine wasn't a particularly hot publication, but that was the genius behind Ejay's plan. I mean, who would claim to be with Details magazine or have been one of the band members in Spin Doctors for that matter? Rolling Stone, sure, GQ, why not? But Details? It was so random that we had to be on the level. The smoke from the Mexican forest fires was more pronounced in San Antonio, so perhaps that somehow aided in our deception, a smokescreen or something. I don't know. I took pictures pretending to be working while Ejay palled around with the bartenders and made sure I took pictures of their establishment for the magazine. We headed off from one bar to the next with more people in tow each time. At some point the limo broke down, but one of the bartenders hooked us up with a city bus. The next morning, we were dropped off at the Travis Heights house by a San Antonio VIA city bus.

But at the end of the day, we weren't doing anything particularly egregious. We were just being twenty-something, wasting time with each other while we avoided the topic of what we were going to do with our lives.

Helpful hints about Austin: Part II

-Eeyore's Birthday
Right off Lamar is Pease Park. It's a great location for scenic strolls, playing disc golf, and of course having a gathering of thousands of hippies playing in drum circles, bathing in the limestone bottom streams, general frolicking and body painting. What else would you expect from a festival called Eeyore's birthday? I consider this the last pleasant weather celebration before Austin enters the "You got to be freaking kidding me" kind of heat which lasts from mid May until mid-October. So, if you want to paint your body in Technicolor and spin around in wildflowers, but you don't want to sweat it all off, might I suggest Eeyore's birthday?

-ACL Fest
Bring a Camelbak, fill it with ice and nothing else. You will be grateful you did after a couple of hours. Also, do not wear anything you have any attachment to. That is especially true for footwear.

-SXSW: A Confession
I'm going to tell you something, and frankly I don't know how you will react. The truth of the matter is I don't care for live music. "Whaa?" you gasp. "But Chris, you moved to the live music capital of the world!" Don't you think I know that? Every March I have to cede my personal space at my favorite coffeehouses, restaurants and grocery stores to accommodate the rush of musicians, film makers, techies and their fans who have come to participate in South By Southwest. That's fine and all; I can handle the longer lines for a couple of weeks. But the problem is that I am expected to participate in the action. Even when I

was in Senator Monkey and the Funkicrats, I just wanted to get out of the crowd afterwards and go somewhere sane. It's not that I didn't see live shows in Austin. That's physically impossible. One cannot actually live in Austin without seeing a minimum of eight live shows a year. It's in the city charter. Besides, Ejay was the lead singer of Fist Dive, remember? I had to go to some of his shows for house morale. I guess what it comes down to is this: I like the idea of being in the live music capital of the world, but not actually having to go through the ordeal of live music. I would enjoy the technology shows, but you already know my issue with that.

-The Stevie Ray Vaughan statue
On the south side of the Town Lake trail between South 1st and Lamar stands a statue of Stevie Ray Vaughan. People come to pay homage to the gifted guitarist who went Buddy Holly on us back in 1990. Most leave flowers, some fit a cigarette between the statue's fingers, and some leave a beer. About that last item: It's kind of a massive sign of disrespect to the man. He was a recovering alcoholic and was fortunate enough to die sober. So, the next time you see someone place a beer in the Stevie Ray Vaughan's statue's hand, please be a trooper and appropriately chastise the ass clown for his ignorance.

11

Oh! Well . . . that explains it

Summer 1998

Helmut said he needed me to take another test. I felt another bout of déjà vu as the words came out of his mouth. I couldn't tell if it was the actual phenomenon or if this was the result of having a nearly identical situation not too long ago. I knew the drill. I walked over to my space and saw the sad little school desk waiting for me. Helmut handed me the test, and with as much indignity as a contract bike messenger could muster, I snatched the booklet and Scantron test from him. This time, Helmut got the message. He gave me a sympathetic look and walked off.

The test didn't bother with cursory questions this time. In fact, the first page had only one question.

-Did you get sober for this?
   A. Yes
   B. No
   C. I'm still trying to figure that one out

I felt a rage welling up inside me. It was one of those self-righteous, justified kinds of rages, my favorite type. I pried myself out of the school desk and stormed over to the scrawny man.

"You can call Logos and get another errand boy." I flung the Scantron and stormed off towards the door bringing on the melodrama seen only on *Melrose Place*. If I had a drink in my hand to throw . . . I figured I might get fired for walking off the job. Then again, I might have a good lawsuit for these assholes piecing together details of my personal life to craft some elaborate joke. There had to be some EEO or workplace harassment thing in what they were doing.

Helmut chased after me. "Chris! Please wait! You don't understand."

"The hell I don't. You're goofing on the retard bike messenger. You have no idea what a violation . . . You think you're all that and a bag of chips and y'all can do this to a loser like myself . . ."

"You aren't a loser. You're the Chris. And you don't understand what we're trying to do here."

"What does that even mean, anyway, 'the Chris?' Why did you take advantage of me like this? I might have talked about my sobriety to you guys, but it was . . ." I was shaking I was so livid. I was never coy about my sobriety. I didn't really see the need for the anonymity part in AA until this moment. I finally realized how stupid I was for revealing so much personal information about myself so freely. There are some things that should remain private, because there are people out there who will take advantage of you and your openness. My fists were clenched. I didn't know who I wanted to deck more: Helmut or myself.

Helmut tried to calm me down. "Chris, you never mentioned a thing about your sobriety to us."

"Oh, really?"

"You never mentioned your sobriety, just as you never mentioned that your fourth grade teacher Mrs. Brown was your favorite teacher."

"Yeah, about that. How in the hell did you find out about her?" I could never figure that one out.

Helmut ignored the question. I noticed the others stopped doing whatever it was they were doing and walked over to me.

Helmut continued. "You also never mentioned that you constantly doubt yourself, where you're going in life."

"Oh come on, Helmut! I'm twenty-five years old! All of us don't know where we're going or what to do. We all ask ourselves that."

"Not in the way you do. They worry about careers. Yours is about something more fundamental, not only jobs, though you do tend to confuse the two. You worry about your purpose. You always did, ever since you were a child. It consumed you."

The room got silent as he continued. "You tell me if I'm wrong. You constantly doubt your abilities and you worry that there is some flaw in your character that will sabotage you in the end, the same flaw that nearly destroyed you with your drinking. And here's the really crazy part: You got sober, and overcame so many obstacles and yet you don't dare give yourself any of the credit out of an irrational fear that it will somehow set you up for a relapse."

He was absolutely right. I never voiced it out loud, but that was precisely how I thought about it.

And then Helmut landed the bombshell. "You had a vision; it was brought on by smoking a cigarette dipped in something—I'm not sure what. You saw yourself years from now having done nothing with your life . . . where you squandered every advantage and became a loser."

Suddenly, I found it difficult to breathe . . . I might have told them about being a recovering alcoholic. I might have even told them about me having a foot fetish. But I never told *anyone* about that vision. That was something too personal even for me to share.

My lips trembled. "How d . . . did you know?"

"You are Chris Jung. You got sober on December 11, 1993 after crashing into the back of an SUV. The only thought you had at that moment was if you hurt anyone. You say that you're afraid of clowns, but you're really afraid of garden gnomes, but there's nothing funny about that."

Helmut moved uncomfortably close, but then again, he was reciting some of my most intimate thought, so what's too close? He then put a hand on my shoulder.

"We know these things about you, Chris, because it is what we were able to reconstruct from the forensics."

"The forensics? Of what?"

"The destruction of all existence."

"Um, the destruction of all existence?" I repeated. Everyone in the Stubb Foundation, all twenty-four of them encircled me. "Wow, that's pretty, um, bad, um isn't it?"

"Yes. It is very bad." He stepped back and rubbed his face. "Chris, we didn't want to reveal this until we had confirmed we were in the right reality."

He walked me over to one of the TVs that was connected to one of the PCs. "Chris, there's something we need to discuss, but I am finding difficulty where to begin, because that's kind of a relative term. So let's just start by saying that all existence will be consumed into a vortex on October 26, 1999. Everything that ever was or ever will be will cease to exist or have existed."

I nodded. "1999, huh?" I tried to make myself look smart. "Um, this doesn't have anything to do with Y2K, does it?"

"No, Chris, it doesn't. It's a little more than that."

Helmut proceeded to show me a really impressive Power Point presentation. "This is reality, Chris. You have consciousness. You exist. Can you imagine non-existence?"

I understood what he was asking. He wasn't asking about imagining the world without me. He was asking about non-existence. What was it like to not exist?

"No, I've tried." Actually, it's something I tried doing since I was a kid. I tried to imagine nothing, but it was always blackness, and that was a color. Also, I tried to imagine not being, but my conscious efforts were a contradiction.

"Non-existence is a dangerous thing. Some try to imagine a vacuum, but the vacuum of space is *not* nothing. The vacuum of space is far from non-existence. In fact it is the foundation of existence. It is the fabric of space/time complete with echoes of events that occurred and will occur."

I was partially with him. Admittedly, I always thought of nothing as a vacuum but I nodded as he went on. Helmut went up to the blank TV screen and starting drawing. I realized that it was some sort of neat interface with a pen that interacted with the screen. From all the techno crap strewn about the office, I knew Stubb Foundation was developing something. This must have been one of them. Helmut wrote this down:

- Existence is expressed in the vessel that is the universe.
- The universe is comprised of the entire tapestry of space/time and all constituent holdings to include matter, dark matter, and antimatter.
- Multiverse is an implied subset of the universe.
- The universe has a variety of realities, which in popular culture are referred to as "parallel universes" or "alternate realities." They share the same space but are different expressions of existence.

I thought about this last item: the realities or parallel universes. I don't know how this popped into my head, but it did. "So, in a sense all of these realities, they're like all the colors or hues that make up white light."

Helmut thought it over. "'Hues,' I like that. That's not literal of course, but yes, the realities expressed as different 'hues' as you call it share the same space. So, instead of an alternate reality where the Nazis won, there is a *hue* where the Nazis won. That hue co-exists with this hue we live in where the Allies won. Some hues have a limited life and are subsumed back into a dominant hue. Understand?"

"I think so."

"Consciousness is imbued within the fabric of space/time itself. Your brain's chemical reactions do their job to allow you to perceive as a human, but consciousness is part of existence and vice versa and it goes beyond what you commonly understand as consciousness. Existence and consciousness are the same. There can be no consciousness without existence and vice versa."

That made sense, at least the part about there cannot be consciousness without existence. It redefined the Cartesian relational duality between subject and object, but I could see it.

"Existence is all of the universe with all of its temporal realities or *hues* and consciousness is imbued in the very fabric of space/time itself which makes up existence," Helmut reiterated. "The problem is that somebody in the future disturbs existence."

"In October 1999?"

"No," Helmut said struggling to explain. "Actually, it happens 326 million years from now when what could reasonably be called one of humanity's descendants . . . let's call them species A46 . . ."

"Why that? Why not call them by the name they refer to themselves?"

"Because the current technology doesn't allow me to."

"What?"

"Look," he said exasperated, "we'll call them A46, okay?"

"Fine. So, what did the A46s do?"

"They created nothing."

"Ah . . . like they failed to create . . ."

"No, Chris. They created *nothing*. Nothing is dangerous. Existence, the universe conceived nothing, and that had a cascading effect. The pocket of nothing created is unstable and needs an anchor and we have determined that it anchors here on October 26, 1999. And when it does, then this never happened."

I sat there for a moment in the comfy if smelly La-Z-Boy Hank usually sat in putting all of this together. A normal person would either think these people mad or that they were jerking me around. After the emotional exchange with them about my sobriety, I came to the belief that they weren't jerking me around. Were they crazy? Well, they knew details of my thoughts that I never shared, some not even with myself. If they were crazy, then I was, too. But I decided to throw something out to get that question of sanity out of the way. The problem was even if Helmut said yes, I would still believe him. I asked anyway.

"So, are you from the future, or from another hue?"

"Neither. I was born on August 4, 1971. And I grew up in the same timeline as you."

"Okay, so you're aliens?"

"Hector's from El Salvador, but I don't think that's what you mean. No, we are home-grown homo sapiens born in the traditional linear tradition."

Humans rarely referred to themselves as "homo sapiens" or having been born in the "traditional linear tradition," but that effectively answered the sanity question on my end.

"Okay, so how do you know this if it occurred in the future?"

"We were born to know this. We were born to resolve this."

I thought about my next question. "So, you, all of you were born to stop this nothing from devouring the universe." I couldn't help but think about that movie I saw repeatedly when I was a kid, *The Neverending Story.*

"Yes."

"And the Stubb Foundation . . . it was created for this purpose."

"Yes, that is why it was created. We found each other, and we established the Stubb Foundation for the sole purpose of reinforcing space/time at the right location at the right time in the right 'hue' as you call it to contain it and prevent the nothing from anchoring . . . to create a patch, as it were."

"Man . . . and I thought you guys were in software design."

"We dabble in a lot of different areas in the high-tech industry. We need capital to accomplish our mission. We also need other companies with the given industrial base to construct what we need of them. And we need you. We know a Chris is, or should I say potentially will be involved in our mission . . . a Chris that shares your memories, your thoughts and we think your pickup truck.

"*Value Menus?*"

Helmut nodded. "We need your help."

"What? To save the universe?

"Yes. Are you busy?"

12

Chris and the amazing multicolored Jell-O mold

Summer 1998

The revelation at the Stubb Foundation was hard to digest. It was even harder to believe. Supposing they were correct, and that 326 million years from now one of our descendants will accidentally unravel all of existence by creating an eight ball of nothing. How could they know that? Furthermore, what could they do about it if this was the case? And if the universe was so smart, why didn't it send some of species A46 to our time to patch the universe? If nothing else, couldn't some alien race in our time with superior technology fly on over and do us all the favor? After all, it's their universe, too. That's what I thought. According to Helmut, species A46 did travel to the late 20th century in a closely related hue and it only strengthened the nothing. And as for aliens, Helmut stated that the mathematical projections showed that the means to patch the universe couldn't involve any alien intervention. I asked why and when Helmut began to speak, my eyes glazed over and then he snapped his fingers. He swore he spoke for two minutes, but I recalled nothing. Apparently, the human brain doesn't register some concepts. Finally, after further prodding on the alien question, Helmut said that every time aliens come to earth, they get roaring drunk, anal probe the natives and mutilate the cattle before having a chance to do anything of value and are recalled back home.

All of this would be entirely too thin to accept except for one thing I couldn't deny: They knew my intimate thoughts. How could they manage that if they were just delusional? Maybe they used some form of hypnosis. I considered that driving home, but then something occurred to me. What were they really trying to do? The universe was poised to be dissolved into nothing, and they saw it as their life's calling to stop it from happening. I'd say that was noble of them. Of all of the cliché mission statements I heard from the multitude of startups I applied to and never heard back from, I never heard one that was so direct. The Stubb Foundation was created to save all existence from annihilation. That certainly shat all over the "revolutionize the way we think of communication" tropes I overheard at beer bashes.

I drove home listening to a cassette of the Gourds, who Fist Dive once opened for, and reflected on everything I learned today. Maybe I should have just left the Stubb Foundation right then. But what could I say? I was flattered. The entire fate of the universe hung in the balance and I was key to saving it. How? I had no idea. They weren't quite sure yet, either. All they knew was that a Chris with my memories in one of the nearby hues (temporal realities, remember?) was involved in patching the fabric of space/time, somewhere within Earth's orbit. I was most likely "the Chris" they were looking for. Now I understood why they called me that. I might be *the* Chris. *Me!* Well, I have to say, that was special, special indeed.

Ejay was getting ready for work at Club Deville and was making Tara a concoction while Stacy drank the rest of the iced coffee in the fridge. I sat them down and I told them what Helmut had just revealed to me. They listened patiently as I tried to explain about this nothing devouring the universe. The problem is that when someone who barely knows anything about a subject tries to explain something they don't really understand, it sounds even stupider than it was in his or her mind.

I finished telling a long and confusing recounting of events. There was a protracted silence until Ejay raised his hand as if he were in school.

"'The Nothing?' Are we talking about *The Neverending Story?*"

I sighed. "No, Ejay, we're not . . ."

"Call my name, Bastian!" Ejay quoted from the 1984 summer hit movie. "I can't! I have to keep my feet on the ground!" he mocked in a kid voice.

"I'm serious, man!"

"I know. I know! And that's why I love you!" Ejay walked downstairs singing "The never ending story, la la la. Hey, there's my luck dragon!"

I turned to Stacy. "He's right you know. I'd better come up with a different name for it than 'the nothing.' Knowing my luck, I'll get sued."

Tara looked worried. "Chris, these people could be dangerous."

"Oh come on, Tara. They're harmless."

"Perhaps, but the way you've described them, they sound like some kind of cult."

"I wouldn't call them a cult. They're just eccentric. I mean, they aren't the only company I see who has strange ideas."

"No doubt, but they also aren't claiming that they have exclusive knowledge about the end of the universe. I mean . . . . look, just be really careful, okay?"

I turned to Stacy. She looked at me and said, "Hey, man, whatever works for you. You want to save the world . . ."

"It's the universe, actually. We're saving all of existence," I said proudly.

"Fine. You want to save the universe. I do too. I want to sow the seeds of a revolution to empower people. I say carry on, my wayward son."

I figured none of them truly believed what the Stubb Foundation told me. I wasn't exactly willing to bet my life that they weren't barking mad either. I smiled and headed outside for a smoke. Stacy followed behind me and added with a whisper, "But Tara has a point. Please be careful."

You would think that something as profound as the revelation on Friday would have altered the entire trajectory of my life. Well, it kind of did. I mean, I returned to work Monday and everything seemed normal. They still ordered from Chuys using the proprietary online ordering website. I still picked it up at 10:30. I still sorted through mail and ran jobs. In that sense, things were profoundly the same. But things did change. The shroud of secrecy they had in my presence was lifted. I was in the know now, so to speak. To be honest, whenever Helmut or anyone else there tried to explain how they knew what they knew or what they were doing to save the universe, I would black out. Stella, Shirley, Helmut or Hector or someone else would try to explain something pertaining to the true nature of the universe, and I would be with them for a few seconds but then the next thing I knew they were asking if I was okay. I would follow along right up to "You have heard of string theory . . ." or "so this quantum foam permeates . . ." or "so the universal cohesion is proportional to the paratectonic . . ." It didn't matter, I would always black out. I found it infuriating, because I really did want to know. Despite having no background in math, I loved cosmology and concepts in quantum mechanics. My mom would have us watch *Cosmos* when I was a kid, and I was a total geek for this stuff. So, as much as I didn't have a scientific background, I knew quite a lot for a dilettante. But apparently, my mind wasn't capable of processing what they were trying to teach me. It was like trying to explain the third dimension of space to a creature in a two-dimensional planiverse.

But despite my inherent limitations, this is what I gleaned. Existence, i.e., the universe, is a quivering, not fully solid, Jell-o mold. I say it quivers because, well, contrary to those who subscribe to the block universe idea, things aren't really set.

The hues, or "parallel realities," share the same matter that comprises existence in the time/space Jell-O mold. They borrow matter and space/time to do their thing like a timeshare. The whole quantum uncertainty issue is simply the infinite number of hues making use of the same particles at any given moment. Here's the interesting thing about this: Let's just say you have a cup of iced coffee on your desk. You assume it's always there, but that is not necessarily the case. The particles of the iced coffee are shared in all hues involving an iced coffee. It isn't until you reach for the iced coffee and drink that the hue requires the iced coffee's presence. This hue borrows the particles for you to drink. This is what I mean by timeshare.

That got me thinking about how you lose your keys only to find them minutes later in the same exact spot you just searched. You assume you overlooked it somehow, but perhaps not. And then I thought about my socks in the dryer that go missing from time to time. Is it possible that the vibrations of the undulating dryer cause some sort of quantum flux where an unsuspecting sock is completely thrown from this hue and deposited in some far-off hue, like one where Kennedy wasn't assassinated? There could be all sorts of articles of clothing and mismatched socks strewn about existence. The errant sock I found the other day in the dryer could have been from the hue where Japan never attacked Pearl Harbor, thus delaying the US' entry into World War II until it was too late. Either that or it belonged to Ejay.

Back to the quivering Jell-O mold of existence. It's multicolored. Each color represents a hue. So, these hues share the same space. Maybe the color rustic creme will only exist for a small portion of the mold because sometimes a hue gets subsumed or integrated into another hue. Rustic creme gives up and joins sierra beige. Sometimes a hue will split into two or more tangent hues.

So, that's it. Existence is a quivering, not quite solid, multicolored Jell-O mold where hues share matter and energy like a timeshare. Take hold of that and don't let it go.

Other than coming up with the most reductionist way to describe existence, I more or less left the business of saving the universe to the good folks at the Stubb Foundation. I asked if there was anything I could do right now. All they said was to please be sure to snag some extra chips next time I get lunch, and that they would let me know if there was anything else.

I did contribute one thing to the Stubb Foundation regarding saving the universe. I coined a new term for this "nothing" that threatened to consume existence. The term "nothing" didn't sit right with me, and it wasn't just because it reminded me of that movie. It just seemed . . . I don't know . . . bland. I also didn't like the term "void." Both terms conjured the image of a black abyss, which as you know is actually *something*. But whatever the term would be, I thought to myself, it had to be bereft of qualities. It had to be the absence of . . . *that's it! "Absence."*

Absence of what? That's the point! The term itself is incomplete. I thought of it while riding around McKinney Falls. Excitedly, I raced over to the Stubb Foundation and offered my idea. I was nearly out of breath. McKinney Falls was a trek to Barton Springs Road.

I burst into the Stubb Foundation and announced, "Let's call it . . . Wait for it . . . The Absence!" I said theatrically.

Stella, Hector, Helmut and Sheila shrugged their shoulders. "Yeah, whatever," and went back to staring at the static on the TV screen.

I was so proud. I contributed to the naming of the threat to existence.

The excitement of being part of some grand plan and me giving it a proper name slowly subsided, and I more or less went back to doing what I had been before. That being said, I started to pay careful attention to the correspondence at the Stubb Foundation. Whereas I had earlier chalked up any pickup or delivery as just another run-of-the-mill exchange between one high-tech firm and another, I now saw everyone who worked with the foundation as being part of this grand scheme—whatever it was—to save the universe.

I rifled through the mail, I listened in on calls and I perused documents being delivered to and from the Stubb Foundation, and this is what I gathered about their business dealings. They were major shareholders in dozens of corporations, consortiums and conglomerates. I think they were venture capitalists of sorts, investors as well as owners of dozens of patents that they licensed out. Incidentally, I learned that the software that Rapture uses in protecting computer networks from the Y2K bug is not theirs. In fact, they license it from the Stubb Foundation, which has proprietary rights. The Stubb Foundation was the majority shareholder in Enron and Worldcom. They had their hands in everything, including Circuit City, Pets.com, Linens n Things, Things-N-Shit, you name it. The Stubb Foundation was behind the success of all these giants in the new economy. I briefly considered the possibility that Helmut and company was involved in some crazy financial scheme to inflate the market artificially for some unknown purpose, and then I did the smartest thing. I said, "Don't think about it. You know nothing."

Something in my outlook changed after that revelation. Of course, I would see the universe with a different lens come happy hour that last Friday considering I became privy to the universe and its nemesis the Absence. But it wasn't that alone. I began to suspect things, even the most mundane events, served a purpose. One of the more popular bumper stickers going around the city advised everyone to "commit senseless acts of randomness." I had reluctantly subscribed to that philosophy for a long time. After all, I sort of fell into things, including getting sober and moving to Austin. But after that revelation, I began to suspect that I was being guided somehow. I was far from certain, but it was an itching feeling. I still had no clue what to do with my life, but then something random happened.

13

The random happening

August 1998

My day started out in the usual way. I came into the Stubb Foundation, made the coffee and sorted through the mail, quickly scanning the content when I could to get clues on their dealings. Sheila, Siobahn and Hank were connecting a stereo receiver to a toaster—don't even ask—and Heath was staring at static on a television screen, nothing unusual. Helmut handed me my orders to pick up and deliver. Most of the deliveries were in biking range and given the heat index and dry forecast I would have stood to make a lot of money what with the Stubb Foundation's distance/temperature/precipitation axial chart. Unfortunately, my Kona was out of commission for the moment after I busted the derailleur on a jagged rock. Oh well, I hopped into *Value Menus* and headed off.

The first stop wouldn't have been in cycling range as it was way out in Buda (you pronounce the "u" like "cute" and not like "Buddha"). I looked up the address in the Key Map and drew my route onto a legal pad. Helmut's instruction said I was to wait for a signature from the recipient. I glanced at the recipient's name to find it was none other than Funky Freiburger. It is been said that Alfi "Funky" Freiburger is "world-famous in Austin." Known for his kosher barbecue sauce called Yippie Oy Vey and kosher Tex-Mex sauces, Funky dabbled in a host of things; music, political satire and two runs for governor and one run for the US Senate. He never came close to winning either office, but he did manage to raise the hackles of the established parties for supposedly being a spoiler. Both parties claimed this in the same race, by the way.

I was buzzed into Funky's ranch/office and entered the foyer to find the secretary battling with a commercial espresso machine. I told her I was from the Stubb Foundation to get a signature and she walked me right into Funky's office.

"This gentleman's from the Stubb Foundation."

Funky swiveled in his chair and gestured for me to take a seat. He was engaged in an animated phone conversation.

"Listen, son, I don't care what your boss thinks. If he wants my money he's gonna have to play ball!"

I sat quietly looking around the office that looked more like a hunting lodge. It was a ranch in brush country south of the city, so it seemed appropriate. I tried not to stare at Funky as he argued with whoever was on the other line, but he looked pretty much exactly like he did on the Yippie Oy Vey labels. He had a handlebar mustache and wore a cowboy hat and bolo tie.

"Well, you tell the congressman that I don't exactly like helping that bombastic ass myself, but I have my orders just like he does, and if he doesn't like it, I'm sure he can find someone else to pay for the ads . . . Yeah . . . uh huh . . . . That's what I said." Funky nodded a couple of times. "Okay then . . . glad to hear it. Well, I think we can work with you. Call me on Monday . . . Okay . . . uh huh. Good then. Later."

Funky hung up the phone. "Schmuck."

He shook himself and greeted me. "Howdy, son. You got something for me?"

"Yes, sir." I handed him the documents to sign and I stared at the framed photograph on the desk of him and the secretary with Willie Nelson and Lyle Lovett.

He started going over the paperwork. "So, how's Helmut doing?"

I was surprised. People usually never talked to the messenger. "Me? Yeah, um, he does well . . . you know, for Helmut . . ."

Funky belted out in laughter. "Yeah, he's a strange one, ain't he?" I nodded. "And what's crazy is that he's the most normal of them!"

"That is true."

"Still, I owe that man. He saved my ass."

"Really?"

Funky looked around the expansive room dramatically as if looking for someone eavesdropping and he put his hand to his mouth as he whispered. "Let's just say I had a little ouble-tre with my axes-te. He made it go away"

"Ah," I responded neutrally. I had no idea why Funky was confiding to me, a complete stranger, on what had to be a nefarious dealing between him and Helmut. But then again, I do have a trustworthy face. He took a sip from his cup and made a face. He then hit the intercom button.

"Are you trying to kill me, Janet?"

"Sorry, Funky, what is it this time?"

"The cappuccino . . . it's horrible! Did you try to poison me again?"

"It's not my fault. It's that damned espresso machine!"

I could hear her right outside arguing very casually with her boss. There didn't appear to be a reason to have an intercom between them.

"I just bought that. It's a ten thousand-dollar Lavazza. You shouldn't be having a problem with it whatsoever."

I raised my hand. "Um, Mr. Freiburger?"

"Please, son, call me Funky."

"Okay, Funky. I think I might be able to help. I worked with Lavazza machines before."

We both went out to the foyer and Janet showed me over to the machine. I examined it and then made an espresso. As it poured I immediately saw the problem. I pulled the machine out and adjusted the valves.

"Back in New Orleans I was a barista, and we had a similar machine. Lavazza is great, but you need to adjust for both atmospheric pressure as well as humidity; otherwise, the pull will be too long and be bitter or worse, nutty. Also, the water here is a little soft so you'll want to change the tubes once a year."

I checked the pipe, tested the draw and then made a fresh espresso. This time it was flawless. One ounce with a perfect crema on top. Funky tasted it and patted me on the back.

"Hell, son, you sure make a good espresso."

Funky was so impressed he kept me there while we talked coffee. Turns out he was really into coffee and wanted to expand into the coffee business as his next venture. He appreciated my help and gave me his card. He said he was thinking about opening a coffeehouse and maybe I could manage it. I didn't relish the idea of going back to serving coffee. It was almost as bad as renting cars, but I was polite.

After chatting with Funky and Janet, I headed off to continue my deliveries over to the Texas Secretary of State, the Travis County Courthouse, and one of the downtown dotcoms. I ran into Zeke and Reagan and we bullshitted for awhile and then I went into the downtown Frost Bank location to deposit the foundation's checks. As I was pulling out into the street, someone hit *Value Menus* from behind. I cursed and turned off the engine.

A business man got out of his gargantuan Dodge Canyonero SUV. "Ah, jeeze, sorry. So sorry" he said repeatedly.

"It's fine. I'm okay."

"Damn, man, I'm so sorry."

"Really. It's okay."

I was the one whose vehicle got hit, and yet I was the one calming *him* down. I assessed the damage to *Value Menus*. It was a fender bender, literally. The fender was bent from the minor collision. The guy took a look and smacked his forehead.

"God, I am such an idiot!"

"It's no big deal. Let's just trade insurance information and we can move on with our day."

The guy sucked in air through his teeth. I made a face. "Don't tell me, you bought this nice big suburban assault vehicle but you don't have insurance."

"No, it's not that!" the guy said. "I do. It's just that . . . well, I've been in a lot of these collisions lately ever since I moved here from California." I struggled not to make a snide remark about another stupid Californian in a big SUV.

"If my insurance gets wind of this, they could drop me." He paused. "Could we work this some other way? I'll pay you out of pocket."

Normally, I would automatically reject the offer out of hand. But then he added, "I work at the bank here. I swear I'm not screwing you." He then handed me his card. Josh was the assistant manager at the Frost Bank downtown branch in charge of wire transfers.

"Get an estimate, and I swear I'll pay a hundred over it," he pressed on.

I hemmed and hawed a second before acquiescing. "Okay, fine."

"Great. Thanks." He wrote my name down, got back into his SUV and drove off, jumping a curb as he turned.

I scoffed and carried on.

It was early afternoon when I arrived at the UT campus to pick up a packet from the McCombs School of Business. It was the end of summer and students were beginning to arrive. Parking was a problem, so I ended up far away near one of the liberal arts buildings. I picked up the packet and got back into my truck. I was about to pull out when I saw a lady by her car with the hood up. I don't claim to be a Southern gentleman and the lady was in a safe setting, so I was content to just leave when I noticed she was distressed to the point of crying. I looked at my watch. If I was going to get a free iced latte at my next delivery at iSoar I'd better step on it. Beer bash was on in an hour.

Ignore it, Chris. She'll be fine and it's none of your business. I gritted my teeth. "Damn it!" I turned off the engine and walked over to her.

"Ma'am, do you need assistance?"

The middle-aged woman wiped her tears. "Thanks. But I don't know how you can help unless you know how to start this damned car."

"Sorry, my mechanical skills are limited to changing tires."

"Why now?" she yelled to the Oldsmobile. "The one time I really need you!"

"I can take you somewhere if you need. It's okay, I'm not a creep."

She gave a wry smile. "Thanks, but I need to go to Buda."

If you didn't catch that, the lady just said she needed to go to Buda, though she incorrectly pronounced it "Buddha."

I snickered. "Wow, that's odd. I was in Buda this morning delivering something to Funky Freiburger."

Her jaw dropped. Funky Freiburger was world-famous in Austin, after all.

"I don't believe it," she said.

"I know! And he's a really nice, too."

"No, that's not what I mean." She took a moment to catch her breath. "I have to go to Buda to see Funky Freiburger."

"Really? Wow that is . . . crazy!" For the record, that truly is crazy. "What for, if you don't mind me asking?"

"Oh, it's a long story."

"Well, come on. You can tell me on the way over."

Song on the car stereo: "Laid" by James
Visit www.michaeljuge.com on the *Here We Are Now* page to listen

On the drive back to Buda, Marsha, the lady in distress, filled me in on her dilemma. She was the coordinator for the UT Anthropology Department. Every year they received a huge grant from none other than Funky Freiburger himself. Funky had been a "C" student in high school and was admitted into UT quite by accident. Once he got in, he chose to major in anthropology. There he met his wife, and she gave him the idea to start the kosher barbecue sauce business. He credited his enormous success, in part, to the serendipitous chain of events that got him into UT where he met the love of his life and learned about the Humanities, which he claimed was more important than a business degree. I would disagree with him, but look where he is and look where I am.

In appreciation for his meteoric rise, Funky set up a fund for the Anthropology Department. Every year, Funky donated $100,000 to the department to use as it saw fit, but here's the catch.

"We have to accept one low performer each year," Marsha said.

"A 'low performer'?"

"Yes. You know . . . an applicant whose score on the SAT wasn't particularly impressive or in our case in the graduate program, the GRE score hovered in the average range, had mediocre grades, that sort of thing. As Funky was a low performer himself, he wanted our department to remember to always leave a little room for a 'dark horse'."

"That's sounds really nice of him."

"The only problem is, we screwed up . . . or should I say the new dean of anthropology screwed up."

Marsha explained that her new boss was supposed to select an applicant from the pile of rejects who weren't completely unqualified per se but who were definitely *not* the overachievers who typically applied for the highly distinguished program. Unfortunately, the dean ignored her urgent and sometimes incessant reminders and now, the Friday before orientation, she had received word that Funky had dropped his funding for the year.

"I called as many applicants as I could this morning, but they either didn't answer or had gone into other programs. I tried to get in touch with Funky but he wouldn't take my call. I must explain that I need just a couple of days to get a student in." Marsha clenched her fists. "We really need that money."

And suddenly I had an epiphany. It was like being struck by a . . . uh . . . by a big thing hitting me—I was never too good with analogies. I thought about the infinite hues out there in existence, how events interconnect, where causality and meaning try to meet. I considered the likelihood of today unfolding the way it did, and how remote the chances were of them occurring the way they did. This was a sign, it had to be. The universe might be trying to guide me here.

"You know, Marsha," I said as we took the exit to Buda, "I have a rather unimpressive GRE score and some shitty grades if I don't say so myself . . ."

Needless to say, Marsha was thrilled. I had taken the GRE several months back, in fact. I barely broke a thousand and thanks to my early days in college before I got sober, my cumulative GPA was equally pedestrian, above 2.5 thanks to the last two years of straight A's but less than a 3.0. I even applied to the graduate program at UT in philosophy and was soundly rejected. Oh, I was perfect! I never thought I my mediocrity would come in so handy.

The butter was churning now. Funky was happy to oblige, especially knowing that I was his dark horse beneficiary. The only problem was we needed to wire the funds by the close of business that day. I don't know why . . . it had something to do with matching contributions from a fellowship program. So, Funky had to be there in person at the bank to wire the funds. Unfortunately, the banks were going to close in less than twenty minutes. I was about to panic when I remembered that the universe might be smiling on me today.

"You wouldn't happen do your banking over at Frost Bank by chance . . ."

So, Marsha, Funky and I crammed ourselves into *Value Menus* and raced towards downtown. Funky would have taken us in his Hummer but it was in the shop again—Mercury retrograde he claimed. His other vehicle was a hog. I grabbed the business card Josh, the assistant manager in charge of wire transfers who ran into me this morning, had given me and handed it to Funky. He had a cell phone and dialed for me. I explained it to Josh, told him to not worry about the repairs if he stayed there to do a wire transfer. Josh said he was able to keep the system online to wire transfers only if there was a slowdown in the network that kept the wire transfer in process. Then I had Funky call Helmut, since I was driving. I asked Funky to relay the information about me potentially going to grad school and ask if that messed up their "plans." I certainly wouldn't want my entering graduate school to cause the Absence to strengthen and destroy existence. Sure, the universe was most likely encouraging me to go, but I had to be sure.

Several minutes later, Helmut called back to say that I was good to go; furthermore, the Stubb Foundation created enough congestion on the servers that it would leave a wire transfer in process until we arrived. I used my knowledge of the city streets to weave our way into downtown and the wire transfer successfully went through, effectively enrolling me as a graduate student in anthropology at UT. This was by far one of the most productive days I'd had in years.

14

Course correction

September 1998

Song playing on the jukebox: "Cut Your Hair" by Pavement
Visit www.michaeljuge.com on the *Here We Are Now* page to listen

The Mexican forest fires that had smothered the city the entire summer had finally dissipated. Maybe the smoke just moved to Houston. It was replaced by cigarette smoke inside Waterloo Draft House. As expected of a Friday afternoon, Waterloo was exuberantly packed with college students, young software engineers and at the far corner, me at a table full of overly serious anthropology graduate students. These were my new cohorts for the next two years, three if the student loans didn't pan out and I had to go back to humping it on my Kona and in *Value Menus* again fulltime. The Funky Freiburger Fund wasn't a scholarship, but rather a grant to the department in exchange for admitting a guy such as myself into their program. I was on the hook for the tuition. The Stubb Foundation agreed to hire me directly to work part time, half days three days a week. They even gave me a cell phone. Gone was the Logos-issued beeper.

I had felt like I had been living in the wilderness since graduating college, as though I didn't belong in the real world. I left my college days kicking and screaming, banging on the doors, "Don't throw me out there! I'm not ready! I want to stay home with you guys!" I was right. After two years of taking daily abuse from irate customers at Terminal

Car Rentals and playing Russian roulette on my bike, I really needed to be here. That probably explained my sudden and unexpected urge to help Marsha out by volunteering to be her ringer. I'll admit it. It's not like I had any particular passion for anthropology. Humans were smelly, barbaric and overly-emotional. I should know. I am one, and that description fits me well. But it was the idea of getting out of a rut that inspired me. Grad school was a course correction, a way to redeem my undergraduate GPA, take a timeout and figure out what I was to do with my life—the universe blinking out of existence notwithstanding. What will I do with a masters degree in anthropology? Why anthropology and not something more practical, say an MBA? Details, foolish details. The point was I was back where I belonged. These were my people. Well . . . except that they weren't exactly.

While the Jaegermeister girls were serving body shots a scant ten feet away, I was distracted by this increasingly heated discussion between two of my cohorts.

"Yeah, well, if you read your Chomsky, you would know that the Internet is not going to serve to democratize knowledge, but rather codify Western hegemony," spat out a young lady with intense-looking blue eyes.

The object of the young lady's ire quickly retorted. "And why do you say that, Heather, because you heard it on NPR?"

The others at the table who grasped the substance of the heated argument *oohed*.

"No, Andre. I say that because anyone who spent time actually living among the people instead of drinking martinis at the Intercontinental Hotel would know that at the end of the day, all communication in cyber space is at its core deposited into the Roman alphabet, and therefore all language is made further subservient to the Anglo-patriarchal hierarchy."

"Ah, that is entirely jejune!"

"Jejune?"

"Yes, Heather, jejune."

"You have the temerity to say that I'm being jejune?"

My thoughts veered to Reagan Womack. I wanted my favorite crass shitkicker to come in with two drunk girls from Austin Community

College around his arms and belch, "Let's get our lap dances on, bitches! It's half price at Yellow Rose!" I wanted Zeke to mutter something about the dumb-assed gringo who didn't get the poetry of the street. But I was here with these people discussing . . . well, I really had no idea what they were discussing, to be honest.

Just then a skinny dude with Elvis Costello glasses sat down next to me. He nodded, put on a high-pitched cartoon voice, and said "I'm so high I don't know what's going on!"

I was taken by surprise and wound up laughing so hard I started coughing.

"Whoa there, Chief. You okay?"

"Yeah, just give me a minute." I lit another cigarette and extended my hand to the hip-looking guy. "My name's Chris."

"Hey, Chris. Pleased to meet you. My name's Gary, Gary Hughes."

Gary and I talked for the next few minutes over the noise of the crowd and the bar's speakers playing Pavement, which was battling for attention with the jukebox upstairs playing Freak Nasty. I could tell that Gary and I were going to get along well, especially surrounded by the rest of the anthropology crew. The two of us discussed the declining state of commercial rock since the mid-nineties. Gary had a godlike knowledge of the Indie rock scene, which far surpassed my own. The discussion wound its way around everything not pertaining to anthropology, from movie quotes to indie bands (I feigned knowledge for the most part) to the longevity of *The Simpsons* over *South Park*.

"And let me tell you the worst part about getting hit by a minivan," I boasted, casually bragging about my misadventures as a bike messenger when I glanced across the table and saw a woman who had just sat down.

She was stunning. Even in the dark, smoke-filled bar, I could tell that the woman sitting across the table from me was among the most beautiful women I had set eyes on, and that was saying a lot in Austin, a town teeming with talent. The woman gazed at me with deep brown eyes through librarian glasses; her short reddish-brown hair lightly touching her elegant neck. She wasn't dressed like the other anthropology students, all of whom were dressed as shabbily as possible.

This woman was wearing a suit, an honest to God "I've got to go to court" suit. She reminded me of Agent Dana Scully.

"So, what's the worst part of getting hit by a minivan?"

"What?"

Gary nudged me. "So, what's the worst part?"

I had forgotten the conversation with Gary. I realized that I was staring at her. A cigarette dangled from my mouth stupidly.

"Oh, um . . . man, I totally . . ." I struggled to collect myself. I straightened my ponytail and scanned myself to make sure there was no ketchup on my Flipnotics coffeehouse T-shirt and prepared my opening line to this woman who looked like she belonged somewhere else, like at the Law Office of Taylor, Swift and Lavigne.

Instead of coming up with a seismic opening, I jerked my head with a stiff nod and managed to utter, "Hey."

Her name was Meredith. Meredith Anderson. The moment she spoke her name, I whispered it to myself again and again. It wasn't that I feared forgetting her name; I just didn't know what else to do. I don't need to go into details about how that first encounter went. Truth be told, it was a rushed blur I think in part due to my own frantic and mangled way of socializing with someone way out of my league. But this is what I remember.

"So," she asked, "You're in the anthropology program?"

"Yes, aren't you?" There was a tinge of desperation in my voice. Gary gave me a quizzical look trying to figure if I was okay.

"Yes, and I'm also working on my masters at the LBJ School of Public Affairs."

Meredith had high cheekbones, an oval face. And she had these eyes. I could smell her perfume past the beer and smoke. What in the hell was she doing here? Yes, she was in anthropology. I got that. But what was this lady doing with something as stupid as anthropology?

I ended up asking the dumbest of questions, the question that I hated anyone asking me.

"So, what interested you in anthropology?" I asked.

Through the smoke, the music died down. Meredith took a long moment before answering.

"I've been asking myself that for a while now. I tell myself it will compliment my public affairs degree, but . . ." Her answer was so sincere. "What about you? What interested you in the anthropology program?"

I wanted to be honest. I wanted to say that a random series of events transpired last week precisely so I could meet her. Instead, I answered her honest question with one of my patent, cheap throw aways.

"Well, you know. The judge gave me a choice. It was anthropology or prison."

She laughed, and I was through the moon. Meredith Anderson had the most infectious laugh.

"No, really."

When she looked at me with those eyes, I felt myself utterly disarmed. It was as though she looked into me, I swear. My funny guy façade was just that, a front. I knew I had nothing profound to say. I was about to narc on myself when I was saved by the bell.

Stacy walked up to me and pushed me off my stool, "Sup, biatch?"

15

It's called corporate espionage

September 1998

I was curled up in the human-sized cat's cradle I had made for myself in the far corner at the Stubb Foundation trying to make sense of my reading assignment. I had registered for the following seminars:

-   *The Dialectics of Orientalist Ethnographers*
-   *(Re) Interpretations of Real and Imagined Space*
-   *Gender Identities and the Subjective African Diaspora*
    and my favorite
-   *Eroticism(s) and the Deconstructed Oral Tradition.*

I was thumbing through the dictionary trying to figure out what the hell the course titles meant. I figured I should know before class. The syllabus listed a number of books, all which looked riveting in the same way discussing cabinetry could be riveting. I had a distinct feeling that this was not going to be as easy as undergrad had been. I was in a deep trance when Helmut walked up.

"Hey Chris, you available?"

"Yeah, sure. What's up?"

"I need you to take me to CynerDygm."

I thought that was a little unusual. Unlike most of the others at the Stubb Foundation, Helmut had a driver's license. Most never left the abandoned-looking compound of the Stubb Foundation except for dentist appointments or to attend some conference, or occasionally shop for more sensible clothes at Target when their threads had been worn to the point of losing molecular cohesion. Otherwise, they stayed indoors. At least Helmut got out of the compound a few days a week. He drove the red Saab parked under the building, which is another indicator of someone who is a little off: a Saab. It's just a strange car, you know? I mean, who drove a Saab . . . other than Swedes, of course? So, it was strange that he was asking me to give him a ride. But as they say, "mo money mo problems," so I grabbed my keys.

CynerDygm had taken over the office space of one of the earlier dotcom evolutionary dead ends at the Arboretum. *Value Menus* chugged up the hill and I knew just where to park.

Inside the darkened garage, Helmut pulled out a strange-looking device. The part sticking out looked like a little metal duck's mouth. He turned to me.

"Everyone is upstairs at the beer bash. You go in there and socialize with them."

"That's easy. My friend Stacy is up there now, in fact."

Stacy had recently returned to CynerDygm. Actually, she was still working for Rapture. CynerDygm hired Rapture to patch their computer network with the software they licensed from the Stubb Foundation. I could draw a link chart, but you get the idea. Rapture assigned Stacy to this contract, for as a former CynerDygm employee she knew the systems already.

"Good." He then handed me an earpiece.

"What's this?"

"For while you're up there. If you see anyone going back inside, I need you to say 'Vandelay.'"

"What does it do?"

"It's something we're working on. We might call it a green ear, a red eye or a blue something. I don't know. But I will be able to hear you while I work."

I backed up. "Wait, why do you care if someone goes back inside?" and then I said "duh" to myself. Helmut just gave me a look.

"Dude!" I whispered. I pulled him close. "You want me to participate in some sort of . . ."

"It's called corporate espionage, Chris."

"Yeah, that!"

"Do you have a problem with this?"

I couldn't tell if he was being sarcastic. I didn't think he was. Helmut was the closest to normal of the bunch. Hell, he was normal enough to try and commit corporate espionage if that made any sense.

"Does this have anything to do with trying to save the universe from collapsing into the Absence?"

"Yes."

"You swear you're not shitting me about this? All of existence is really in peril?" I don't know why I was bothering asking him now, standing in the parking garage right before committing what had to be a crime. I just needed assurance, I guess.

He looked at me. "Chris, I am not shitting you. I swear. This is important."

CynerDygm had expanded since Stacy first worked there back in '96. For perspective, that was before Madonna returned from Argentina with a British accent. I found Stacy outside on the expansive balcony at CynerDygm overlooking the Hill Country. It was a typical Friday afternoon. The employees stopped working once the beer whistle was blown promptly at 3 p.m. CynerDygm spared no expense at their weekly beer bashes. They had the best local beers on tap: Shiner, Celis Pale, Dirty Bastard Ale. I tell you as someone who got sober right before the microbrewery explosion; I was tempted from time to time.

I walked past employees of CynerDygm and overheard the conversations.

"Dude, so I'm patching it with 2.4 and she's like, 'Does that work on a Unix?'"

"Serious, yo?"

"Yeah, she is such a 'tard."

"Sup, G!"

"Hey, gangsta!"

"Yo, we've gots to get a negosh going, word?"

"I hear ya, dawg. They say my contract doesn't allow me to go, though."

"Man you are so money, you don't even know!"

"Does your laptop have an Ethernet coupler for DSL?"

"Yeah. They say the zip drive might be corrupted, though."

"Shame. Mine's got a CD burner."

"I get stock options, so when this thing goes IPO, I'm cashing in, man, and that's it! I'm totally getting off this fucking grid!"

"Go home, Dan. You're drunk."

I made my way over to Stacy and I noticed she had her arms around a tall skinny guy with an Abraham Lincoln chin beard. Another great thing about the '90s was the explosion in facial hair experimentations. Just as startups were exploring the uncharted reaches of what the World Wide Web had to offer in commerce, so too, young men were exploring the multitude of facial hair styles no longer hindered by the chains of the previous decade that demanded clean angles.

We had surpassed the Jesus beard and goatee. Men were trying out the Abe Lincoln chin beard, the Stonewall Jackson, the handlebar 'stache, the soul patch, the porn star, the Latin American military junta pencil mustache, the perv, the Burnside sideburns and (my personal favorite) the chinless walrus, aka sideburns meets a mustache but with no hair on the chin. Men were free to go as freaky as they wanted because the '90s gave us something important: irony. If it was ridiculous, we could always claim it to be an ironic gesture.

People were looking at me standing beside Stacy and I realized it was the earpiece they were checking out. In the reflection I noticed it had a blue light on it.

"Wow, nice piece of tech, Chris. That isn't like you," Stacy said.

"Oh, thanks. Um," I started to worry. Why didn't Helmut provide me with a more surreptitious listening device? Certainly, he shouldn't have made it so obvious that it caught people's attention. I started bullshitting as fast as I could. "Um, yeah, the Stubb Foundation has me wear it. It . . . um, it"

I was beginning to sweat but then again, I always sweat, so it didn't matter. And then the perfect lie hit me. "It's connected to my cell phone."

Abraham Lincoln chin beard guy took particular interest. "How so?"

"Oh, I don't know exactly. I'm a total idiot on technology. Right, Stacy? But it has something to do with the RF signal on my cell phone, so I don't have to hold it up to my ear." I once overheard two guys discussing something regarding "RF signals" while waiting to get our oil changed at Espresso Lube.

"It helps when I'm driving."

"Yo, Mark, check this out!" Abraham Lincoln chin beard guy called. More people gathered around me. I soon realized that Helmut used me as bait to lure people away, not just to be a lookout. All these people from around the deck encircled me. I became the center of attention. The DJ even stopped spinning Sublime.

I cleared my throat. "You see?" I pulled out my new Stubb Foundation-issued cell phone, extended the antenna and made a call to Stacy. I figured what I would do is pretend that this red eye, green ear or whatever it was to be called was connected to the cell phone. And it probably wouldn't work, but that wouldn't surprise anyone. Cell phone reception sucked pretty much everywhere back then so it was plausible. I sent the call. To my utter amazement and shock, I heard the dial tone in my ear. When Stacy picked up, I could hear her.

"Holy shit I was right! It works on cell phones!"

People applauded. "Wow, and that's a Stubb Foundation product?"

"Did someone say Stubb Foundation?"

"Hey this guy has a prototype!"

"What do they call it, man?"

I struggled to remember what Helmut called it. *Color and body part.* That's all I knew. "Um, it's a . . . blue . . . tooth."

"A 'blue tooth?'" Abraham Lincoln chin beard guy repeated incredulously.

"Uh huh."

"Blue tooth," everyone around murmured with interest.

The hoopla died down after a while and I was integrated back into a regular person in the crowd, though I was more than just the monkey boy making his rounds now. In fact, people were handing me their cards.

Apparently, the Stubb Foundation was getting a lot of attention in the dotcom world. Techies were getting interested in them, though nobody knew anyone who worked there. The business cards were futile attempts to have me call them if there were any openings at Stubb Foundation. The funny thing about their business cards: Pretty much every last one of them listed their job titles as "consultant," "VP of Research and Development," "Senior VP of integrated vertical marketing" and "marketing director" even though I knew that there couldn't possibly be that many chiefs given the company's size. It couldn't possibly be sustainable, right? I felt a passing déjà vu that lasted a few seconds.

"So," Stacy said, "It was nice meeting your classmates." She made it sound like I was in elementary school again.

"Yeah. Gary's good people." I paused before adding, "and there's Meredith, of course." I tried to sound casual about it, but Stacy hit me on the shoulder rather hard and guffawed.

She turned to her boyfriend. "Oh my God, you should have seen Sugar Ray here smoovin' this business school bird!"

"First of all, Meredith is in the LBJ School of Public Affairs, not business. And second, I was doing fine until you interrupted my groove."

"Oh yes, that was some groove you had. You were absolutely killing it with that prattling of yours. What do you call that move, anyway? The sweaty nervous guy? The rambler?"

Okay, Stacy was absolutely correct, and I knew it. I babbled badly. It's a thing with me and beautiful, intelligent women. Meredith asked Gary what we were discussing. He mentioned the declining state of music at the turn of the decade, I agreed, she disagreed, and then, well, I don't exactly know what happened next. All I remember is that my mouth was dry, my palms were sweating and Stacy jumped in to slap me out of my nervous fugue state. So, no, Stacy wasn't wrong. But I didn't think it was necessary for her to let Honest Abe in on my problems.

Stacy could sense my frustration and she tousled my shaggy hair. "Oh, Chris, dear, I kid 'cause I love. You know that."

"I know."

Just then I heard a crackling on the earpiece. "Okay, Chris, I'm done. Meet me back at your truck."

"Well, I really should be heading out. Smell you later."

I left Stacy and the rest of the employees at CynerDygm outside and headed back down into the parking garage where I found Helmut waiting by *Value Menus*. We didn't say a word the whole way back.

16

Having your ass handed to you
by a guy named Sheldon

September 1998

I bought a thousand dollars worth of books for the seminars and figured I would get around to it on the weekend after orientation. I had been away from school a couple of years, so I knew I should get a head start on the reading. But damn the luck, there was this *X-Files* marathon on SciFi that weekend. I know. You're going to say, "But Chris, you already taped all of *The X-Files* episodes. And you've probably seen each of them a million times over. Why would you waste your weekend like that?" Okay, my answer to that is there's a subtly different experience watching it on broadcast TV. I don't know: It has something to do with the collective unconsciousness of viewers watching the same episode at the same time. I'm sure that Sheila or Hank at the Stubb Foundation would back me up on this.

So I didn't read the first assignment for *(Re) Interpretations of Real and Imagined Space*. It was the first seminar of the week. Who reads an entire book in the first week anyway? Apparently, the entire Department of Anthropology, that's who. I sat down and expected the professor to, I don't know, teach, perhaps? This is how I thought it would go: He or she lectures, I take notes, and that's what you're tested on. Those thousand dollars worth of books? *Pah*, that's just a racket to get their books sold. Well, that's not how it works in grad school. There's still the textbook racket that effectively screws you out of your money, but unlike undergrad, they expect you to read them . . . all of them. Not only that, but you are supposed to have a really trenchant analysis of each of the tomes.

In *(Re) Interpretations of Real and Imagined Space*, I was seated behind Heather and Andre. You remember them. They were the battling anthropologists at Waterloo Draft House. This ended up being a blessing. Although I hadn't read anything and they apparently had, it wasn't a problem. In fact, Heather and Andre sucked the air out of the room, arguing the entire class. At one point, the professor who purportedly taught the class but instead just sat back the entire time held up his hand.

"I'm sure there are others in the room who would like to be part of this conversation, guys." Heather and Andre looked around, and I just shrugged my shoulders, and they went back to it.

In *Eroticism(s) and the Deconstructed Oral Tradition,* to my relief I found Gary sitting in the class. The class was neither erotic nor had it anything to do with anything oral. Total letdown. Like the previous seminar, I was completely clueless. *Gender Identities and the Subjective African Diaspora* was exactly what you think it to be. If you happen to know, please share with the rest of us. The professor in *Gender Identities and the Subjective African Diaspora* was this mildly attractive older German woman, Dr. Neko Niederschlaf, who immediately sensed my hesitation upon walking in the room.

I kept my head low and furiously wrote down notes, mostly words with question marks.

- Post-structuralism (not anything to do with architecture, right?)
- Didactic
- Hegemony
- Discursive
- Panopticon
- ~~Fookoh~~ Foucault . . . is that a dude or another term?
- Dialogics

- "Agency" in the anthropological context
  . . . Oh, and speaking of . . . contextualization
- Architectonic
- Deixis
- Idiolect

Technically, they were speaking English. Yes, English with words used by French post-modernists who figured it was better to massage this bastardized Germanic language with its hard vowels with neglected and forgotten words rather than use terms that would be commonly understood by plebes with a mere bachelors degree who got into the program only by chance.

By the time Thursday rolled around, I knew I was in deep. Back in undergrad, philosophy was a natural fit for me. But maybe it wasn't the subject of philosophy so much as it was the professors who taught it, and I do mean actually *taught* the classes. It was particularly unsettling to realize how out of my depth I was here. I was considering jumping out and getting my money back. I could figure something else for my life, I suppose, right?

Maybe I misread what the universe was trying to tell me. Maybe instead of enrolling in graduate school, I was supposed to work for Funky Freiburger. I don't know. Maybe the universe wasn't telling me anything at all, and maybe I was just reading too much into a coincidence, a big one though it was. I can't tell you how many times religions got started by coincidence. Maybe my desperation and fear of being doomed to that Venetian cream induced-vision drove me to make a rash decision and a huge mistake.

I showed up twenty minutes early for the *Dialectics of Orientalist Ethnographers* seminar. I sat there alone contemplating how I seemed to have to run into another dead end. I'll admit it, despite all of the other areas of my life where I lacked confidence: computers, women, sports, carpentry, shopping for cantaloupe, I could at least say that I was smart, or at the minimum smart enough so that I could bullshit my way through several academically rigorous courses and manage to be an A—student, at least after I got sober.

School was the one thing at which I sort of excelled. After two years of having my ass handed to me in the real world, I concluded I wasn't much of a self-starter or much of a commodity, period. Graduate school had been a sudden and unexpected opportunity thrown my way. It was now unraveling before me. I started to panic. I could walk out of this classroom right now and no one would ever know. I would be spared the embarrassment of failing and people wouldn't even remember this Chris Jung character who showed up to orientation and a few classes the first week. Just walk away and put an end to this. I was about to call it a day before anyone showed up for the next seminar. I couldn't remember the whole name of the course anyway. I stood up and headed towards the door. That is, of course, until Meredith walked in.

So, guess what I did? That's right, I stayed primarily because Meredith Anderson was in the *Dialectics of Orientalist Ethnographers* seminar. Dressed in crisp business attire, she sat down across from me. What could I do? As Reagan would say, I "nutted up" and buckled down to study. I hate reading. I hate reading material I don't understand even more. I bought a thesaurus and started transcribing the books from post-modern into English, deciphering the best I could. The Stubb Foundation was the best place for me to study. The Travis Heights home was a den of chaos right now. Ejay was into playing gangsta rap, while Tara rebutted him with her world music. Meanwhile, Stacy was hosting the Greens meetings. I really didn't think I would be able to digest the amount of material at the Travis Heights house.

The Stubb Foundation was also accommodating. They set up a discarded desktop in my corner. Sheila even purchased the software license to interface with the UT network so I could check my new UT student email account. Sheila showed me how to send and receive emails. I got the basics. For the most part, the Stubb Foundation was quiet. The associates tended to gaggle around the other side of the office. I would come in before or after class, run my errands and read.

My efforts, inspired by the presence of the beautiful Meredith Anderson, didn't bring about a sea change in my output as I expected after seeing so many movies like *Back to School* or *Soul Man*. In the *(Re)*

Interpretations of Real and Imagined Space seminar, I chose to do a book review of Edward Said's *Orientalism*. That was met with a thud by most of the class. Reviewing Edward Said and that book in particular is the anthropological equivalent of walking into a guitar store and trying out a Gibson by playing "Stairway to Heaven." You just don't take the most obvious work, by the founding father of post-modern cultural theory, and question what it meant.

The reception was met with, "typical white male ignorati." That was from Sheldon, a white male who made me look ethnic in comparison.

"Wow, it's Max Weber. I think your pith helmet and gin are waiting for you back at your master-planned community where you can watch your Fox News and football." In the liberal arts world that would be considered an epic burn.

I came away after having my ass handed to me by a guy named Sheldon with one kernel of knowledge: Hollywood lies.

17

A field trip to the crooked E

October 1998

Popular Halloween costume: Monica Lewinsky in soiled blue dress

I came in to work to find the entire crew of the Stubb Foundation crowded around a table pouring bottles of shampoo into Petri dishes. They were passing them around while each inspected the goo, holding it up to the light and smelling it. I swear these guys were seriously off, and you would never know by the smell of them that they had any interest in bathing, much less scrutinizing shampoo for whatever purpose they had in mind.

Helmut was the only one who acknowledged my presence. The others were too enthralled by the shampoo. "We need to go to Houston," he said.

"Houston? What is it?"

"It's a big city with an IKEA and a mediocre baseball team, but that's not important."

Helmut was dressed up . . . well, dressed up by Stubb Foundation standards. He wore a clean button-down shirt over slacks that were clean albeit way too big and a sharkskin sports coat which totally didn't match.

"You brought *Value Menus* today, right?"

"Yes, I did. But, um."

"What is it?"

"Well, *Value Menus* is getting a little hinky. It can barely climb the hills, and there's this strange burning smell."

"Oh, we can't have that, the Chris," added Stella, one of the members who always wore flannel shirts. "*Value Menus* must be in working condition on October 26th."

"That is true," Helmut added, "but we also need it to have between 192,000 and 196,000 miles on that date, and last I checked it stood at only 180,000 miles."

None of this made any sense to me, but I learned not to try to understand. Helmut then turned to me. "Can it make it?"

"I think so."

"We'll replace the engine as soon as we return."

"The engine? Uh, Helmut I can't afford . . ."

"I said 'we.' The Stubb Foundation will be paying for *Value Menus'* engine."

"Oh." I thought a moment. "But doesn't that mess with your calculation of mileage?"

"Why would it? The odometer needs to read between 192,000 and 196,000 miles. The engine running *Value Menus* is inconsequential to the composite quantum foam formula."

"Right."

Song we agreed to play on the drive over:
"Doll Parts" by Hole
Visit **www.michaeljuge.com** on the *Here We Are Now* page to listen

I couldn't keep quiet during the entire drive over to Houston. Silence is unsettling to me for some reason. It's like I somehow failed in socializing. But awkward silence wasn't the only reason I couldn't stay quiet. There were just so many questions I wanted to ask Helmut, like:

- This whole thing about a quantity of Absence devouring all of existence . . . is that still happening?
- How does the universe work again?

- Do you by chance have a paper on Pierre Bourdieu handy from one of the other hues, maybe in the alternate reality where I flourish as a graduate student?
- Would borrowing said paper from my other self in another hue be considered plagiarism?

I rifled through my tape collection and we agreed on Hole, a guilty pleasure of mine. The hills became less pronounced and gave way to gentle inclines and declines as we headed east on Highway 71. It sort of reminded me of my initial drive from New Orleans to Austin years ago, but in reverse.

"So, how is it that you and the others know about this event?" I asked after an hour's silence.

Helmut smiled. "Chris, we've tried to explain this to you a few times over."

"Yeah, I know, and every time you try to explain, you or someone else starts vomiting some verbiage and I black out. I swear you're worse than my *Re-interpretations of Real and Imagined Space* class."

"You shouldn't feel bad. Your reaction is no different from ninety-nine percent of humanity. We're discussing concepts that cannot be conceived with your order of intelligence."

"My order of intelligence?"

"Again, no offense. You are very smart as an individual," he said and then I started feeling this déjà vu again as he spoke. I tried to ignore that unsettling feeling that we were in this exact discussion before in this exact place.

"Are you saying you're some kind of alien?"

"Of course not. And we already went through that, too. I am human."

"But you're of an 'order of intelligence' beyond us mere humans."

"Not alone I am not. Together, all twenty-four of us, we become an order of intelligence far greater than we were separately, far greater than the combined intelligence of twenty-four people even."

"Ah, kind of like the Borg."

"Yes, something like the Borg. We touch the sea of consciousness that is existence. We can only do that as a collective."

"No shit?"

"No shit."

There was a pause. Then he continued. "I want you to look out the window."

"Helmut, I'm driving."

"Just do it, please."

"Okay. I'm doing it."

"And what do you see?"

"I see us passing by trees, other cars and stuff."

"You know what I see? I see time slowing down as you and I accelerate to get around that Volkswagen Beetle. I see the Beetle getting smaller not just in perspective, but literally, and I see *Value Menus* elongating slightly. The trees are experiencing time a little faster than me. I see gravity is slightly less warped at the top of that hill than it is down here."

I knew about Einstein's theory of general relativity. Any philosophy major worth his or her weight in water had to have studied some physics, especially the evolution from Newtonian physics to Einsteinian physics all the way to the erratic quantum mechanics.

"You're discussing general relativity. The speed of light is constant no matter from which perspective you're viewing; therefore, everything else, space and time must be relative."

"That is one way of looking at it. In addition, I see other vehicles potentially sharing the same space as us from nearby hues."

The déjà vu finally ended just then and I felt as though it never happened.

"But do you know why the universe follows this one rule about light, why all space and time seem to bend and curve, expand and contract to accommodate the law that light will always travel 186,000 miles per second?"

"No, not really."

"Because, light has no age. Light doesn't get old. It doesn't atrophy. How can that be, you ask. Because, light is the manifest of consciousness. Light just exists. It just is. And that is true consci . . ."

"Chris?"

I slammed on the brakes though I didn't need to. Thank God there wasn't a car behind me. My heart was racing.

"You blacked out again," Helmut said.

I checked the rearview mirror and did a check around to make sure I didn't hit anything.

"I guess we shouldn't discuss anything like that while driving, huh?"

Houston went on forever. We had entered the outskirts 30 miles back and were still in the suburbs. We were now stuck in traffic somewhere between Beltway 8 and the 610 Loop. There were a lot of emergency vehicles trying to pass through. I presume it was a collision that shut down the I-10 eastbound. I briefly thought about the idea of inventing a device that would tell you about traffic conditions. It would be a GPS map like the military had but in your car. Or even better! On your cell phone. *Right. A cell phone that has maps and shows traffic conditions? Yeah, get off the crack pipe, Chris.*

We were literally parked on the I-10. It would be relatively safe if I happened to black out, so I asked. "Okay. What's up with the shampoo?"

"We are working on developing a patch to reinforce space/time."

"And you're making the patch with Prell?"

Helmut snorted. "We're working on an analeptic quantum . . . look, I shouldn't get into details; you're driving. But let's just say that we are trying to leverage ourselves to be in a hue that will be the most compliant with our formula."

"That quantum foam . . . thing?"

"Exactly. Our current technological development limits our abilities."

"As opposed to species A46?"

"That's right. But we've been combing through the clues. There is a means that can seal a rift and contain the Absence."

"Why can't species A46 do it? They're more advanced."

"We've been through this, Chris. They can't because they didn't."

That sounded like circular logic if I ever heard. "Are you saying that we're pre-destined?"

"What? Of course not. Quantum mechanics already invalidated the pre-deterministic model of existence. I thought you already knew that."

"Well, duh. Who doesn't know that?" I got nothing from him on that, so I pressed on,

"But, I mean . . . well, you sound awfully certain that since species A46, didn't, they won't; and therefore it can't happen. It sounds relatively unalterable."

"We move through hues, Chris, so there are a variety of choices and possibilities. We are working on moving to the right hue. But of all the hues we've uncovered in the quantum resonance, we haven't encountered one where species A46 stopped the Absence they created."

"Hmm, isn't that odd?"

"Yes. Yes, it is odd indeed. There should be an endless number of hues to include a possibility where A46 doesn't create the Absence and a hue where they do but they stop it on their own."

"But there isn't."

"Nope."

"So, there aren't an infinite number of hues, are there?"

"No. There aren't, not anymore." Helmut said mordantly.

"Oh." I suddenly felt claustrophobic in the traffic snarl.

"There are a finite number of hues now—beyond calculation, but finite, and it is decreasing."

"Ah, so the options to stop it are decreasing too. That's a problem, isn't it?"

"Yes it is."

The headquarters at Enron was imposing and futuristic-looking. The "crooked E," as it was called by some for its logo, was one of the largest energy companies in the country, providing power to entire states. The monolithic main structure reflected the image of anyone trying to look in, sort of like a skyscraper-sized highway patrolman's silver shades. You try to see the man, but all you see is the distorted image of yourself staring back at you shitting bricks as he asks rhetorically if you knew how fast you were going. I parked *Value Menus* out front. The reflection of the beat-up jalopy from the mirrored windows of the lobby made the pickup truck somehow look even more clownish. Men in suits walked up. I was about to roll down my window and explain I would park legally in a moment, and that I was just dropping off when they opened the door for Helmut.

"Right this way, Mr. Spankmeister."

"My driver will be joining me," he said.

"Of course, sir. Very good." The man who looked like he had stools larger than Helmut politely addressed me. "You can leave the keys with me, sir. We'll have it washed up and ready for when you return."

Shocked, I looked to Helmut, who simply gestured for me to relax. *Value Menus* was my most valuable possession. The Kelley Blue Book value had the '86 Toyota pickup with 186,000 miles somewhere around $800. I figured these guys wouldn't drive off with it, so I handed over the keys and ran to catch up with Helmut and his entourage. This was something to see. Here were all of these executives dressed in the finest suits riding in the elevator with Helmut and me, referring to Helmut with his scraggly beard, unkempt ponytail and mismatching sharkskin jacket and daddy's pants with extreme deference. In fact, I've never seen Helmut so in command.

"Mr. Spankmeister, I think you will like what we've done, sir."

"I hope so," Helmut responded rather sternly.

The elevator went to the top floor. We walked outside onto the roof of the skyscraper, where a helicopter was waiting for us. I wondered why they couldn't fly Helmut directly over from Austin. Why in the hell was I here? If nothing else, why didn't we just drive to wherever we were going instead of coming to Enron first? Helmut, the executives with the security detail and I climbed into the chopper and we were handed headsets.

"We should be at the site in ten minutes."

"Excellent." I saw Helmut steepling his fingers carnivorously as he said that.

The helicopter ferried us over downtown and headed south. We passed by the medical district and landed on top of the roof of a building with the Compaq logo. As we were escorted down into the building, I overheard the executives discussing matters with Helmut.

"We've been having difficulty getting passage of the amendment through the legislature. We've encountered more resistance than we initially expected."

"You didn't add it in as a rider?"

"We did, sir, just like you suggested. But it somehow hit their radar anyhow."

Helmut stroked his beard as we walked down the corridor. "Okay, just include it as a Y2K fee, rather than amending the current laws."

"Do you foresee a problem with the Y2K bug?"

"No. We've licensed the patch software on half the networks in the US. But I need that power available in less than a year. You will have it?"

"Oh, yes sir. Definitely."

"Good. Now, let's see what your subsidiary has been working on."

We walked past several Compaq employees and rows upon rows of mainframes and several clean rooms with folks dressed in protective garb to keep silicon chips free of human hair, skin, bacteria and whatnot.

We were escorted out of the main building to an adjunct facility located on the same grounds as the Compaq building but the logo in front of this building said "Tyrel Laboratories." Whereas Compaq was clearly a technology business, Tyrel Laboratories seemed to be working in the field of biomedical research, as evidenced by the awards placed on the walls and the negative pressurized research labs warning of bio containment levels. In some of the labs people wore scrubs, gloves and masks. In the labs labeled "Bio Level 4," they wore full chem/bio suits connected to air pumps. That gave me the heebie-jeebies. I sure hoped we weren't going into one of those labs. I couldn't help but think about the scene in the *X-Files* where this idiot scientist was examining a body and got sprayed by this alien virus that formed into a boil on the carcass. Eew . . . Nevermind.

We walked inside a dimly lit vault where one of the employees wearing a Tyrel Laboratories lab coat handed Helmut a cube-shaped case. Helmut placed it on top of a table and opened it. Inside, there looked to be a clear plastic jar filled with orange shampoo—Herbal Essence, if I was not mistaken. Helmut took out a laptop from his messenger bag and connected it to the base of the cube casing that held the jar of shampoo-looking goo, which had these connection ports. The orange goo glowed to life as Helmut typed quickly in his laptop and flickered as he typed commands. I saw a wolfish smile through his scraggly beard.

Helmut cradled the case containing the jar of glowing orange goo in his lap as we drove back to Austin. I tried to avoid bumps. Enron had washed *Value Menus* as they said they would. We stayed quiet for much of the ride home. To be honest, Helmut kind of freaked me out. Those big wig executives treated him with not only utmost respect, but also some amount of fear. What was it about him that inspired that reaction? Did he know something about each of the executives? Did he provide information about the future? I tried to get the Gestalt of their conversations. I really couldn't follow too well. All I knew is that Enron was having some sort of trouble getting a state government on board to do something it wanted, Helmut was offering advice on what to do. Whatever he was telling them to do, the Enron executives were quick to take his advice.

I wanted to know what this entire trip to Houston was about. What was Enron's role in the scheme to save the universe? What was a technology company like Compaq and a biomedical research company like Tyrel Laboratories doing together? What was in the damned jar?

"It's not shampoo is it?" I said, breaking the silence as we passed La Grange.

Helmut chuckled. "The gel? No."

"May I ask what it is then? Please don't say it's a bio weapon."

"No, it's not a bio weapon."

"So, what is it?"

"It's a data-infused poly-carbon neural peptide."

"Ah." After a moment, "And what's that?"

"It's a prototype for an organic CPU. We need to run quantum computing in order to calibrate the analeptic quantum teleological foam in the precise hue. Binary coding doesn't work. DNA can accomplish quantum computations far more efficiently than silicon chips can."

"So, it comes with Windows 98?"

He grinned. "The combined computing memory of all of computers on earth is roughly 80 terabytes of information. All of those mainframes you saw inside Compaq that are tied with controlling nodes to conduct distributive computing? They are the most advanced commercially available computers, and can process up to one teraflop of information per second. This organic CPU can process an order of ten to the twenty of that when it's asleep. We're talking about processing capabilities that go well beyond petaflops."

Most of that escaped me. "Wow. So, you bought Tyrel's prototype?"

"There would be no prototype to buy had we not spurred the industrial base that could produce this CPU here. We helped to establish the foundational research, we funded ventures, and we hold stake in companies that can produce what we need. And that includes this CPU."

I thought about that for a few moments and considered my next question. "So, those companies . . . are you in charge of them?"

"They serve their purpose for the cause. We need a nonexistent technology to be produced; furthermore, we have extraordinary energy demands on that day to come, so we promoted those companies that could serve us in that mission."

As I passed up other vehicles, I couldn't help but think what Helmut told me about how he viewed the world around him. To him, that lady I just passed is experiencing time differently. And we are all driving through curved space. It looked like a straight line to me. But to Helmut, there are long, winding curves through several dimensions. And there were vehicles I couldn't see because I could only see one hue. I was not part of this timeless light. My brain was stuck in three dimensions of space, one dimension of time and it could only comprehend one reality, one hue. I could not be part of this collective consciousness that Helmut and the Stubb Foundation used to commiserate with each other. Hell, I couldn't even figure out what the hell a bunch of students were talking about in class even though I've read the same material as they did.

"You know what your problem is?" Helmut asked rhetorically as if we were having a conversation about me and my problems. Maybe we were and I blacked out again. I turned down the radio playing Everlast.

"Yeah, what's my problem?"

"You're approaching it entirely wrong. You're under the mistaken impression that what you're studying is a science."

I didn't bother asking him how he knew I was thinking about my studies. I doubt it was a lucky guess, and I hoped he didn't have insight to the stray dirty thoughts I have about Agent Dana Scully from time to time.

"Anthropology is a science, Helmut."

"Anthropology is indeed a science, but you're not studying anthropology, are you? You're not conducting research into physiological evolution. You're not even studying the cultures, are you?"

"What do you mean? The classes specifically talked about ethnographies, African diasporas and shit like that."

"And are they actually talking about the cultures? Are they actually studying the civilizations? Are they quantifying, are they qualifying? Are they laying down a hypothesis and conducting research to either prove or disprove the results?"

"Well, no. Of course not. That's kind of imperialist to presume we can study others without being tainted by our own lens of perception, tainted by our own cultural prejudices."

"I appreciate that, Chris. I understand a thing or two about relativity, but that does not mean you forego the efforts of study." He paused for a moment. "Don't you see, Chris? You're looking for a scientific method in a group of people who have given up on doing research. Call it 'imperialistic.' Call it whatever you like. The truth is you're lost because you think you're studying anthropology, but in reality you all are just talking about talking."

18

You go, girl!

December 1998

I thought about what Helmut said, and had taken it to heart. Before our trip to Houston, I was of the mind to just mimic what I read and heard in class. I was attempting to piece together a paper that would find general acceptance in the *Dialectics of Orientalist Ethnographers* seminar. It was a collection of some articles about Zar cults in the Sudan. It was dull, it was plodding; I believe Heather would describe it as "jejune." It included all those cute fifty-cent words I heard being thrown about. But I tore it up, so to speak, and started a new file. I had a wild hair up my ass and decided on something completely different.

It was the end of the semester, and term papers were due. I was sitting nervously in the *Dialectics of Orientalist Ethnographers* seminar. It was my day to present my paper. Margaret entered and sat down next to me. I liked her. She sort of found her way into anthropology randomly the way I did. She wanted to go to law school, but she needed to find a way to redeem her undergraduate GPA. Then Sheldon strutted in. You wouldn't take a second look at him on the street, but in the Anthropology Department, Sheldon was like the captain of the football team. He had a condescending attitude to go with it. A few more people came in and then Meredith Anderson took her seat. I gave her a shy glance. She nodded curtly and I thought I saw a smile behind those librarian frames.

Margaret delivered her paper. Sheldon asked some questions, more than the professor himself. And then it was my turn. My paper was entitled *Derrida, Please*, which was a critique not of Jacques Derrida so much as the declining use of research in anthropology in general. I argued that while post-structuralism was an important reminder of the limits of studying others, the rejection of conducting research out of fear of looking paternalistic or colonialist was intellectual cowardice. I read through my notes having drunk two dirty chai lattes (chai powder mixed with skim milk hot or cold and a double shot of espresso. I recommend adding a dash of cinnamon). When I finished, Sheldon was there waiting to pounce.

"I'm having trouble sorting through your monosyllabic drivel, but let me ask you this. You seem to adhere to a substantialist paradigm and reject the recuperative indissolubility in postulating a reactionary agenda."

"Um, I don't think that's what I . . ."

"It's apparent that you're mystified by the recontextualization of oppositional imperatives that post-modernism instructs in the narrative moment."

Okay, I had no idea what the hell he was saying now. But I reckoned Sheldon misinterpreted the point of my paper. I was about to stutter something when suddenly I saw Meredith raise her hand.

"I think your point is valid, Chris. I especially like your analysis showing the lack of quantitative surveys and interviews in the most recent ethnographies we read." Meredith was dressed in business attire as always. Her glasses slipped as she spoke. I loved the way she said my name.

"That is entirely irrelevant!" Sheldon interrupted. "Chris, is complicitous in defamiliarizing and appropriating a vacuous thesis."

"'Complicitous'?" she repeated. "Do you mean *complicit*?"

"In the profane vernacular."

"No, in actual normal spoken English," she retorted. I stepped back as Meredith continued.

"Let me ask you, Sheldon. Could you please repeat your criticism of Chris' paper using words that I can understand, because frankly, I suspect you're playing Mad Libs, stringing a bunch of abused terms together. His paper wasn't ground-breaking, per se, but it certainly had more substance than your paper on 'Conjunctive Fetishsizings of the Discursive Space.' What does that mean, anyway?"

"Well, apparently neither you nor Chris have internalized the precepts of post-modernism."

An unsettling quiet had cast over the classroom as Sheldon and Meredith faced off. I wasn't even anywhere near the action. I huddled down, making myself fit inside the podium as they did the proverbial saunter from opposite ends of the room. A tumbleweed trundled by. In the distance, I could hear a dog barking.

Meredith pushed her glasses back into place, and took a breath.

"I went to UT so that I could expand my focus in public affairs with anthropology. I came here specifically so that I could learn about other cultures, learn how humanity in its diversity can perceive things differently and apply that to my work in a governmental agency or an NGO for the purpose of serving the people. I want to do right by indigenous people, Sheldon. That's precisely why I chose the dual program. I could have gone to Georgetown in global strategic studies, but I didn't. I thought that by coming here I would learn how I could be of service by understanding the worldview of others and incorporating that in how we do things. But in three semesters, I haven't learned one useful thing in this department."

"Applied anthropology, how repulsive," Sheldon spat out.

"You revile anything with a practical application, Sheldon, even when the purpose is to benefit the peoples you purportedly study. But you don't study other cultures, do you? You chide research, you reject anything approaching utility in the real world to help people in their real lives. You do that because it is easy to stand aside and not take responsibility for anything in this world. Instead you expend oxygen talking in circles. Do you plan to do anything with your vast knowledge other than one day teaching others how to think like you?"

Sheldon opened his mouth to speak, but nothing came out.

You ever see those cheesy '80s films, you know, where someone gives a rousing speech, and afterwards someone claps his hands, slowly at first? He is joined by another and then another. And in the next moment the entire field, hallway, or stadium is awash in enthusiastic applause. Yeah. It didn't happen here, sad to say, but there was a close second as Margaret raised her hand meekly.

"So, it's not just me?"

Coffee Part II: What makes a good coffeehouse?

-Independently owned or local chain coffeehouses are preferred. Coffee is more likely to have a unique flavor (hopefully a pleasant one) and there is a higher chance an independent coffeehouse has some character versus a national chain.

-Are you a coffeehouse or a restaurant? Make up your mind. Some coffeehouses try to be everything to everyone. The problem is, once you decide to be about sandwiches and serving breakfast, you've put coffee on the back burner. It has to do with mood. Can't you do both well? No, apparently it is a physical impossibility. Unlike quantum entanglement, which allows a particle to be two things simultaneously, it does not extend to the coffeehouse/restaurant concept, though it's fine if you double as a bakery.

-Not too many rooms. I love coffeehouses that are set in actual houses. There is no better way to convey authenticity and give your coffeehouse a unique feel than to be located in a house. It's much better than a unit at a strip mall. That being said, you're going to want to knock down most of the walls that separate the rooms. This isn't a bordello. You want to give your coffeehouse an open, expansive feel. You do not want to compartmentalize your customers off too much. A separate nook or so is great, but in the end you want to encourage people to see people, not be off in some random room.

-Lefties make better coffee. I prefer to keep my politics and coffee separate much in the way I prefer to separate food from sexploitation. That's why I don't do Hooters. But if it is a politically charged coffeehouse, at least it should be far enough left of center that it should make you feel slightly stuffy. If you go into a coffeehouse and see bills about some upcoming WTO protest or an LGBT singles night, then there is a better chance the barista with the tats and piercings has pride in his coffeehouse's street cred, and part of that cred has to do with making quality coffee. I've been to a couple of coffeehouses reminding me that I haven't been saved and that I am going to hell. I have to say I have found the coffee to be equally unenlightened and depressing at those places.

-Music. No classic rock. Seriously, I don't get into the coffee drinking mood with "Slow Ride." Classical? I don't know. Are you just looking to not offend? Limited doses of that. Pop radio? Get out. Seriously, just hand the keys over to the bank and get out. Maybe you should let the barista DJ, but I must stress this: keep the volume down! It's not a freaking nightclub. People want to be able to converse without having to scream a conversation.

19

Getting my Mojo's on

December 1998

Mojo's Coffeehouse was one of my favorites in Austin. It met all of my criteria and it sold T-shirts. Exams were over and Gary and I were sitting outside Mojo's discussing tomorrow's party. We were waiting for Ejay to get out from his exams. I felt relatively confident that my term papers, while not earth-shattering works, were adequate. Meredith coming to my defense reassured me that I was standing on solid enough ground academically. It was December, meaning it was pleasantly cool in Austin, cool enough that I could wear a jacket and not sweat.

Earlier, I had told Gary about the presentation in the *Dialectics of Orientalist Ethnographers* seminar and Meredith's epic smackdown. I thanked her profusely and then I realized I was babbling something about these crazy kids these days with their hair and their clothes. And then I sort of ran off. I'm a playa like that. Word had gotten around about her defense of actual research and she sort of became a cult hero not only in anthropology but throughout many of the area studies departments.

"So, it's cool if Mindy comes," Gary asked.

"Yeah, invite whoever you want. What program is she in again?" I lit another cigarette from my previous one. I get into chain smoking when I drink coffee and socialize.

"Mindy? She's in Middle Eastern Studies."

I snickered. Raquel graduated in Middle Eastern Studies, too.

"What?" he asked.

"Nothing. So, you were saying about this Chemical Brothers?"

Gary handed me a CD. "I think you'll like them. You mentioned liking Prodigy, so I figured you might like them, as well. Also, there's the Crystal Method."

Gary was like Rain Man on indie music, but he wasn't a dick about it. You know how some people throw names of obscure bands in a direct attempt to one-up you, or they'll say how they loved a band until they achieved mainstream recognition and then they completely disowned them? Gary wasn't like that at all. He admitted to loving Oasis, Pearl Jam and Nirvana as much as he loved Brian Jonestown Massacre, Grand Champeen, Ween, Nation of Ulysses and some dude named Elliott Smith. Gary wasn't posing as anything. He just loved music. So, I deferred to him to help me expand my horizons beyond my limited collection of '60s psychedelic and mainstream grunge.

"You know, I would love to record this onto another CD instead of cassette. I have a feeling that one day, I'm going to have this huge collection of cassettes and there's going to be something that basically renders it obsolete."

"I thought the CD had effectively replaced the cassette, chief."

"Not really. I mean, you can't record onto a CD yet."

Gary scoffed. "Um, yes you can. It's called 'burning.'"

"Oh, so that's what Stacy meant! She meant recording music onto a CD."

"Yeah, what do you think she meant?" he asked, confused, before looking up. "Sup, G?"

Ejay walked up and gave me a noogie from behind.

"'Sup, mutha trucka!" He and Gary gave each other the standard man hug.

"How did it go?" I asked, referring to Ejay's final exam.

He shrugged his shoulders. "No surprises. Glad it's over so I can put my focus back into other matters of state . . . and speaking of which, you ready for the party?"

"Yeah, looking forward to it. And thanks for helping set it up."

"Ah, it's my pleasure. You deserve it. We're really proud of you, man, really proud. And to celebrate, I'm going to get wasted."

"That's really sweet, Ejay. You are indeed a gentleman and a scholar." He tipped his imaginary hat to me.

The three of us bullshitted over the next several minutes, discussing what Ejay was going to provide for the party while Gary offered to bring some of his vinyl. Ejay and I discussed the latest *X-Files* episode where Mulder and Scully went to investigate a house that was rumored to be haunted by two lovers who committed suicide during Christmas 1918. Naturally, this was the Christmas episode. The two agents got separated inside the house and were visited by psychoanalyzing ghosts who deconstructed the neurosis that drove Scully to stick with Mulder despite assuring her loneliness and the neurosis that drove Mulder closer to insanity.

Ejay was of the opinion that Mulder and Scully should have hooked up during that episode. I couldn't disagree more. "The lack of a sexual relationship is what is so hot about them," I argued.

Chris Carter was a genius, not by the stories he wrote so much as the dynamic between Mulder and Scully he so carefully developed. There was a subtle sexual tension, *subtle* being the key word. That's precisely what made it so arousing! In fact, during the first the first few seasons, Scully was dressed sort of frumpy and had an unflattering haircut. Yet, you knew—every nerd like me knew—that Scully was hot! Don't sex her up. Don't make her a Barbie. Don't have her wear a bunch of makeup, stilettos and skimpy outfits. No! I wanted Scully to be that sharp, strong and detached professional woman who dressed in a way that left enough to the imagination. Less is more. I made a passionate case to Ejay, ironically using some of the verbiage I learned in anthropology. My dissertation on *the X-Files'* understated sensuality far surpassed anything I had written in graduate school thus far.

We were soon joined by Tara, who had forgotten to pay her rent and raced to pay Ejay back. She sat down with us and we soon were the dominant crowd on the patio. I had another iced coffee with yet another espresso shot for good measure.

Song playing at Mojo's:
"All Tomorrow's Parties" By Los Tres
Visit www.michaeljuge.com on the *Here We Are Now* page to listen

As we conversed, my eyes wandered next door to Pangaea, a clothing boutique. It's one of those places Tara frequented to buy yoga mats and earth-tone blouses supposedly imported from Africa but probably made in China. Through the window I saw an attractive woman in jeans and a black leather jacket holding an orange dress up to a mirror. She had short bobbed reddish-brown hair. She almost looked like . . . and then I realized it was her. It was Meredith.

"Hey, Chris. You coming or what?"

"Pardon?"

Gary was putting out his cigarette to join Ejay and Tara who were already walking away. "Haven't you been paying attention? Tara just gave us tickets to see *Austin City Limits*! Let's go!"

Getting tickets to an *Austin City Limits* show wasn't a matter of money. You couldn't get tickets to *Austin City Limits*. It was a near impossibility. However Tara scored tickets, a near miracle. Perhaps it was a prize in one of the robot warrior matches. Hillary was unstoppable. I gazed through the window watching Meredith putting the sleeves to her wrist to inspect the rough fit in front of the mirror. Meredith was beautiful, heavenly. I'm running out of adjectives here. And that black leather jacket and jeans . . . I'd never seen her dressed down before.

But Tara had tickets to Austin *freaking* City Limits! Hell, Johnny Cash could be playing for all I knew!

"Give me the ticket. I'll meet you."

"Tara's got them. Let's go!"

Tara and Ejay were now across the street.

"Don't worry about it. I'll catch up with you."

Gary gave me a pained look and ran off to join the others. I suddenly felt another déjà vu come on. I didn't know what I was going to do, how I was going to approach her. I mean, there is no reasonable excuse for me to walk into Pangaea. My eyes followed her as she handed the sales lady the dress and the woman boxed it up for her. I had to make a decision. Should I be outside pretending to be walking just as she left the store, or should I take my chances that she'll . . . . *Oh, crap! She's walking out!*

Meredith exited the boutique and took a left. The déjà vu waned as I got up ready to race towards Mojo's exit, but then she walked towards me. She was immersed in thought looking for something in her purse. This was my moment. Out of ideas, I pulled the old bump into her routine.

"Oh, sorry! I didn't . . . Meredith?"

"Oh, hi, Chris. I didn't see where I was heading. I thought this was the entrance to Half Price Books."

"Really? Wow. It's like two blocks that way." *Why in the hell did I say that?* "But, um, hey, while you're here, would you like to sit for some coffee . . . or you know, whatever?" I winced. "It's no big deal."

God, why do I do this?

"Umm, sure."

"Great! . . . I mean, cool."

In my defense, I was already flying on three espressos and two iced coffees. Even a normal person would be fidgety. Hell, a normal person would be in the hospital. But if I'm going to be really honest, I'd probably spaz out even without the dangerously high level of caffeine in my system. Meredith and I walked inside. She ordered a Fruitopia and I decided on Italian soda for myself rather than risk another caffeinated beverage.

"So, um, will you be able to make it to the party tomorrow?"

Last week I went to Kinkos and made these flyers and handed them to my friends, friendly acquaintances and, of course, Meredith.

"Yes. I emailed my RSVP. You didn't get it?"

"Oh, I don't check my email that often."

That was an understatement. I hardly knew I had an email account. But her answer absolutely delighted me. She was coming to the party! *Calm the hell down, Chris.* I was desperately afraid I would start babbling. I chose my next words carefully.

"Well, I'm really glad you'll be coming. It will be a hoot." *When in the hell do you ever say "hoot," Chris? Never mind. Keep going.* "We're going to have a full spread, so don't worry about dinner. We're going to play Twister and do a little break dancing."

"Oh. That sounds . . . interesting."

Meredith apparently didn't get the *Ghostbusters* reference. Word of advice. Girls don't do movie quotes. You see, guys interpret reality through movie quotes. If I say, "How am I funny? Do I amuse you? What am I a clown to you?" guys will automatically:

A. understand that I am quoting from *Goodfellas* and
B. interpret that I either totally appreciate being seen as a funny guy or resent it in some subaltern state.

You can't assume that with women. *Oh . . . Now I get post-modernism!*

I quickly recovered. "Sorry, it's an inside joke. Hey, I really appreciate the cromulent way you handed Sheldon his ass," I said adding a word I heard Principal Skinner using on *The Simpsons* to sound smart.

"Oh, it was my pleasure. I was happy to defend your critique of the declining state of anthropological research. It really digs in my craw how some cultural theorists have hijacked legitimate research and derided it as somehow being imperialist. Don't get me wrong, I have enormous respect for post structuralism as balance to the earlier paternalism of Weber and Meade, but what the state of anthropology has devolved into is a self-obsessed collection of academics who have no concern other than self-promotion. They don't care about people, just publishing."

She was so passionate in her defense of my paper, but it wasn't my paper so much. Personally, I thought she ascribed more meaning to my paper than I had written down. My paper was merely a platform for her to verbalize what had been brewing under the surface for some time. She was earnest about wanting to do something that would make a difference for humanity. For her, anthropology just wasn't some intellectual exercise; it was meant to serve a purpose, hopefully for the betterment of humanity.

Meredith shook off her frustration of the Anthropology department. "So, your birthday party tomorrow . . . how old will you be?"

"Five."

She giggled. "No seriously."

"It's not my biological birthday actually. It's my sobriety birthday. I'm five years sober."

"Oh," she responded positively. "That's really wonderful. So tomorrow you'll be sober five years?"

"Officially my sobriety date is December 11th of '93, but with exams and all, I figured it was best to hold off a week."

"I see. But I'm confused. You say you're celebrating your sobriety, but the flyer says that the 'booze' is free."

I smiled. "Yeah, it's sort of a tradition that some of my friends started last year, which I guess isn't much of a tradition yet. When my buddies Zeke and Reagan learned about my sobriety date, they decided to celebrate by getting wasted in my honor."

"In front of you? That's not really nice."

"No, it's not like that at all. I paid for the booze."

"Really?"

"Well, I got sober in New Orleans in college. That first year was tough but after that, well, frankly as long as I have my coffee, I'm perfectly content."

Meredith considered that. "Well, that is something new, a kegger to celebrate sobriety."

We chuckled at her observation and I tried not to stare into her beautiful brown eyes too stupidly. I did my best not to study the shape of her lips, the way her short reddish brown hair touched her long neck. I tried to not get distracted by her heavenly tenor voice or the perfume she wore.

"So, if you don't mind me asking, how did you come to get sober?"

"I'm from New Orleans. It was either become a recovering alcoholic or stay a practicing alcoholic."

"Come on. Don't do that."

"Do what?"

"Jokes. You don't need to always entertain people, Chris."

God, she saw right through me. I didn't even realize that's what I did, but it was true.

"I'm sorry," she added. "If it's too personal . . ."

"No. Not at all. I mean, I wouldn't be throwing a kegger for my sobriety if I was too shy to talk about it."

I lit a cigarette. "I'm an alcoholic. It doesn't really matter how I became one. For some it's genetics. Me, I sort of backed myself into it. The result is the same."

I told her my story. I didn't lace it with needless humor or any other of the things I tended to do. I just told her what happened, what it was like, and how I found my way into AA. I told her about my grizzled sponsor Aidan and my best friend Stacy. We laughed at some of the stories I told about some of the antics in that first year sober. For once, I wasn't blowing it with babbling. I maintained something called "composure."

I then asked Meredith about herself. She told me that she was from Wisconsin. She obtained her bachelor's in anthropology from American University and was a year younger than my 25 going on 26 years. I asked her questions because I wanted to know her. I wanted to know about the world she grew up in, how it was that she was this alluring woman talking to me now. And I loved hearing her speak. I noticed that she spoke very distinctly. She *really* enunciated. Maybe it was a Wisconsin thing. I tried to detect a hint of an accent, but there was none to be had other than *not* saying "y'all" and speaking very proper English. The blouse under her black leather jacket had what I think was some cat fur on it. Her glasses were ill-fitting, because they slipped from her nose often.

As we conversed, I idly thought about if there was a hue where she didn't accidentally walk up to Mojo's or if there was a hue where I didn't look through the window into Pangaea. We wouldn't be here talking right now. There was a hue where I didn't get into the Anthropology program. Would we ever meet then?

I didn't want our "coffee talk" to end. But she had errands to run, and I, well, I had to get out now while I was doing fine.

"So, you'll be there tomorrow night?"

"I certainly will. I might have to leave a bit early as I have an early flight back home the next day, but it sounds like it will be fun."

20

The five-year sobriety kegger

December 1998

My five-year sobriety birthday party followed the standard Travis Heights house pattern. Stacy brought over some anarchists along with the Greens. Cliff and Reagan were shotgunning beers while Ejay had one of his girlfriends tend bar. Meanwhile, he and Tara argued over whose turn it was to DJ. Ejay put on Wu Tang Clan using the speakers from his room when Tara finished setting up on the deck the military-grade PSYOPS stereo weapon prototype, which I believe was now banned by the UN. She put on Afro Celt Sound System and it completely drowned out Wu Tang Clan. The inhumanly low bass made everyone feel the urge to defecate, so she agreed to turn it down a notch.

Gary arrived with his crew. They were the graduate students he talked about from the other disciplines at UT. There was his roommate Albert who was in economics and his girlfriend in library sciences. Gary then introduced me to Mindy and we talked outside while Gary set up to take over the DJing. It would finally bring peace between Ejay and Tara. Their feud wasn't bitter, more fun really. I was nervously waiting to see if Meredith would show up and how it would go. I decided to ease up on the coffee lest I get too wired.

"We love you, Chris!" slurred Reagan as he and Cliff shotgunned another beer and threw the cans into the yard below.

"Yeah, man! Thank God you're sober, yo!" slurred Cliff, who was sitting on the rail of the deck then fell over and tumbled down the hill.

Zeke just shook his head. "Fool" It sounded more like "foo" to me.

Gary approached. "Hey chief, any requests?"

I handed him one of my cassettes.

He looked at it and smiled. "*Meddle*? Nice! I haven't heard old school Pink Floyd in years."

Ejay, Tara and I banded together and you can guess what happened next. We started talking about Raquel while Stacy scoffed, "Raquel's rejects going at it again."

"She once stripped a deer down using a jagged rock and then made a salad using its hooves as tongs!" Tara boasted.

"This one time we went camping, and she spotted an emu. Most glorious-looking bird I've ever seen. Well, Raquel was jealous, you see. So she gutted the poor thing, dressed herself in the carcass and reared the baby chicks till they were full grown, about two years. She then convinced her emu children to hunt any bird that threatened her place as the queen."

"She once gave birth while pole dancing and she took home $50,000 in tips that night."

"Her favorite movie is the made for TV miniseries *The Thorn Birds* starring Richard Chamberlain and Rachel Ward."

"Raquel once donated plasma but they accidentally pumped back the platelets of a crocodile."

This went on for a while between the three of us, but then something unexpected happened. Mindy approached.

"Are you talking about Raquel Colman?"

"We sure are."

"I know her!"

"Here's to Raquel!" we all cheered. "The best damned sniper former stripper in the IDF!"

Song on the military-grade stereo:
"Possession" by Sarah McLachlan

Visit www.michaeljuge.com on the *Here We Are Now* page to listen

I peeled my way out of the tales of Raquel when I saw Meredith come outside to join the party. I know I'm prone to dramatizing, so take this with a grain of salt, but I swear as Meredith descended the steps, there was a gust of wind, her reddish hair danced in the breeze. The music immediately switched from Primus to a sultry song by Sarah McLachlan, and I noticed that she was wearing the orange flowing dress she had bought yesterday from Pangaea. When Meredith caught sight of me and smiled, I swore I lost my own name.

Stacy sidled up to me and whispered, "So, she made it."

Reagan rubbed his hands together mischievously. I turned to him. "Reagan, just be cool."

"Hey, it's me."

I didn't know if I should greet her with a hug, a kiss or a handshake. We settled on an awkward man hug with a kiss on her forehead.

"Wow, that's a lovely dress."

"Thanks, and happy birthday." Meredith handed me a present. Nobody else brought presents, nor had I expected them to. I took the present from her, touching her fingers briefly.

"Aw, that's really sweet of you." I opened it. It was a book, a *Sock Puppet Explanations* series on post-modernism. It was perfect, though I wished I had a copy at the beginning of the semester. I realized that we had been standing there for almost a minute with Stacy, Zeke, Tara, Reagan, Gary and Ejay surrounding the two of us when it occurred to me to do what is customary.

"Meredith, I'd like you to meet my friends. People this is Meredith."

I was momentarily frightened by the thought that the circle would collectively say, "So you're Meredith!" or "Oh, we've heard so much about you!" Fortunately, my friends were merciful with me.

I made the individual introductions and proceeded to spend the rest of the evening doing an intricate ballet of socializing with Meredith and then pulling myself away so that it didn't appear as though I was glomming onto her. There was a fine line between indicating one's interest in someone and being clingy. I had no idea what that line looked like and where it was.

Ejay handed champagne flutes out to everyone save for Stacy and me and gave a toast. The party ramped up as the kegs were tapped, a great celebration of five years of sobriety.

I couldn't help but keep tabs on Meredith even though I tried to keep my distance. Some of us moved back inside and went upstairs to the living room.

Reagan was sitting on the couch with Meredith. I was going to try to interject myself when Stacy pulled me back.

"Just relax, Chris."

Meredith seemed perfectly at ease with Reagan and was asking him all sorts of questions. I busied myself getting to know Gary's friends Mindy and Albert. My anthropology colleague Margaret was dancing with Cliff to PM Dawn's rendition of "True" and getting completely wasted.

Meredith got up from the couch and asked me, "Where have you been all evening?"

"Oh" I stuttered. *Shit, I kept too much distance this time. Idiot!* "Well, you know, keeping everyone entertained. But how are you doing?"

"I like your friends. They're very friendly."

"I'm glad to hear that. I hope Reagan wasn't being pushy or anything."

"Him? No, he's harmless."

"How about I refresh your drink?"

"Oh, I have to go. I have an early flight tomorrow."

"That's right." I tried to think of something else to say. "Wow, well, it was great to see you. I'm really glad you showed up."

"Of course."

There was a prolonged moment before she indicated towards the door holding her keys. "Well, I should . . ."

"Yeah. Have a good one." *What?! 'Have a good one?' What is she? Your dry cleaner?*

After she left, I didn't exactly feel like picking up a drink per se, but if I weren't a recovering alcoholic I would have had a drink to swallow a missed opportunity like that. The rest of the evening, Gary, Mindy, Margaret and I compared notes about who was more full of shit in their papers while Ejay's band came over and started practicing around 1 a.m. The cops came, Margaret threw up. We figured that would do for the evening.

1999

Well-known pre-'90s references to 1999
- Space: 1999 aired 1975-1977
- *1999* by Prince and the Revolution released 1982
- *2001: A Space Odyssey* released 1968 (Second scene on the moon in 1999)

Greatest let downs in 1999
- *Star Wars Episode I*
- The rise of Kid Rock

Most common terms in 1999
- "Y2K"
- "Millennium" (as in the turn of the millennium which was to technically take place in 2001, not the TV show)
- "Did you get the memo?"
- "Sounds like someone has the case of the Mondays."
- Pretty much any line from *Office Space*
- "Hella cool" (popularized by the character Cartman on *South Park*)
- "Bling"
- "IPO"
- "We're an Internet consultancy"
- "I'll cut you!"

Drunkest national leader
- Boris Yeltsin of the Russian Federation

Entertainer who mainstreamed the Catholic high school jail bait look:
- Britney Spears

21

Beyond a case of the Mondays

January 1999

1999 had finally arrived. It was a significant year for the world at large, not just for us at the Stubb Foundation who were in the know about the fate of all existence potentially succumbing to the Absence on October 26th. I remember being a kid in the early '80s thinking about what it would be like in 1999. I did have some sense when I was 10. I didn't expect hovercrafts. I knew we would still be driving around in lame-assed land-bound cars. I did, however, hope that we would have gone to Mars, though. Hell, I figured we would at least have returned to the Moon, right? Apparently, I didn't count on that the biggest stumbling block to manned space exploration would be a lack national will without the Soviets to compete against.

But while I was playing my *Stars Wars* action figures with my *GI Joes*, I thought about where I would be. Would I have a Tom Selleck mustache, because my mom always said it made him so handsome? Would I be a successful surgeon, a rock star, a secret agent who killed bad guys for the government, an insurance defense attorney? Would Mohawks be standard by then, sported by presidents and school principals? Would punk be considered soft jazz in 1999?

1999 was a year of much anticipation for everyone of age to appreciate it. And it wasn't just the release of *Star Wars Episode I* we were eagerly anticipating either. As the ball dropped and 1998 gave way to 1999, all of us on some level thought about what a significant moment it had to be. For me, I was hanging with Stacy and Tara at Club DeVille while Ejay tended bar. I was the beard "boyfriend" for Tara, and I was good at it. Tara was between girlfriends and she didn't want to have to constantly say, "Thanks, but I swing for the other team" to eager young men.

Counting down I felt this apprehension. "10, 9, 8 . . ." This was going to be the year, wasn't it? "5,4 . . ." Great things or quite literally nothing. "2 . . . 1 . . ." Snap. New Year's arrived. It was 1999. Whatever was to come I had better do it this year and I had better not screw it up. While others were kissing each other and screaming their heads off, I stared into the TV, my gut clenching. Maybe it was because I woke up that New Year's Eve having that damned vision replaying itself in my head again. It really stuck with me.

There was more chatter about Y2K. I turned on the TV and saw Tom Brokaw discuss some concern over this pesky computer programming that could cause havoc if not addressed. Stacy just scoffed. She had been patching networks for Rapture for some time now, so she knew the ins and outs of Y2K.

Every so often Ejay would tease me. "So, the end of the world is coming, huh? You're the Chris, so don't fuck it up and erase reality."

"Ha, ha. Thanks, Ejay."

Ejay invariably would lower his voice to imitate the narrator in the movie trailers. "In a world where a simple courier is all that stands between tomorrow and oblivion . . . one man, one truck . . ."

"It's getting old Ejay . . ."

"Chris Jung *is* . . . Chris Jung *in* . . . *Special Delivery to Neverwhere!*"

"I'm serious, man!"

I sometimes regretted telling my housemates about the Stubb Foundation's revelation to me. Some part of me still held some shred of doubt, maintaining that there had to be some logical explanation for how they knew my inner thoughts that I hadn't considered yet. What Helmut and the others said about existence . . . It couldn't be *really* happening, right? 1999 would come and go as uneventfully as the years before and years to come . . . and they will come. They can't be right.

But the truth was that jaunt over to Houston last October really bothered me. There was no way that these respectable captains of industry would kowtow and kiss the ring of a scrawny computer geek-looking guy like Helmut Spankmeister, not unless he was a lot more than he appeared to be. That brought to mind those instructions he gave them. Helmut was ordering them to do stuff with governments and he talked about needing some extraordinary amount of energy, and there was that organic goo . . . that organic CPU! And the hues . . . there were no longer an infinite number of hues. That didn't mean a thing to anybody else, but it disturbed the hell out of me.

Beyond the possibility that the declining number of hues meant that the Absence was devouring existence, it conjured a deep-seated fear about free will I'd had since I was a kid. Even in the good old days before the Absence when there were infinite hues, there were infinite versions of me doing certain things, making certain decisions. Did that really mean that I was acting on free will, or was it just a convenient way of saying since every possible incarnation happened, by definition I make every possible decision and could not *not* make every possible decision available? I was then compelled to both get sober and not get sober, because all realities, all hues are real. How am I really "deciding" anything then? Am I just going through the motions and existing, forced to decide something because it's the hue where I am duty-bound by quantum entanglement to decide to go right because in the other hue I took a left? As I thought about it while doing deliveries on my Kona, I nearly got plastered by the opening door of a minivan.

And if I have free will, whether or not there were infinite hues, what will become of me? Am I really going to get my shit together, or will I just continue to just make a series of desperate decisions, never really knowing what it is that is my best course, my best hue? Will I guide myself to my best hue? I couldn't decide which was more frightening: not having free will or having free will but being an incompetent jackass when it came making life decisions.

I called my sponsor Aidan and unloaded my thoughts and fears. He patiently listened. I could hear him hacking a lung in the background and light another cigarette while I discussed my existential crisis. It made me reconsider my own addiction to smoking. Aidan's response was that I was being self-absorbed again, that I needed to do more 12 step work. He was right, of course. He also suggested I cut down to three iced coffees a day.

I spent winter break working fulltime at the Stubb Foundation. The mood had changed since New Year's. There was more activity. The members were more serious and insular than their usual charming selves. I lurked around the office trying to get clues as to what was going on. I didn't know what exactly, but something was up. Also, there were more wires and circuits stapled to the walls. Helmut had me go on repeated runs downtown on my Kona. And then I had to drive back and forth from all these technology companies in the west hills. Fortunately, with *Value Menus'* new engine, I was confident it wouldn't break down on me. The new year brought enormous prosperity to a lot of these startups who were hopeful that they would be purchased by IBM, Motorola, HP or any number of other established Fortune 500 companies.

"Let's take a drive," Helmut said. I had just returned from my morning downtown runs and was slouching in Hank's La-Z-Boy watching Jerry Springer on one of the portable TVs he tended to cradle in the crook of his arm. We got into *Value Menus* and drove over to the Greenbelt entrance at this office park off of the 360 between Lamar and Mopac. Helmut didn't say a word during the whole drive, which wasn't unusual, but something was bothering him. When we parked, I followed him down the trail to the dried creek bed of Barton Creek. It would be a raging stream by April if it rained this winter. I felt another passing sense of déjà vu as we quietly walked down to the creek.

"That's funny, Helmut never takes me on nature walks," I said aloud, hoping to break the increasingly unsettling silence.

He turned around stopped. "There's a chance you need to die."

What?! He just ups and says something like that? I froze. I couldn't say anything for several seconds. Finally, I calmly replied, "Really? Wow, that's . . . . that's a pickle now, isn't?"

"We don't know, Chris, but we've been sifting through the hues. *Value Menus* needs to be there, and yet there is some indication that the Chris is not supposed to be around on that date."

"And you learned this . . . how? You and the rest of the Stubb Foundation had some powwow, did your mind meld or whatever and came to this conclusion?"

"Well, we now have the help of our organic CPU."

"Great. So, a computer is telling you that I have to die?"

Just then a couple walked by. I figured that this wasn't the first time they heard something like that in Austin.

"We don't know. Don't you see? We're trying to figure it out."

"You said I was 'the Chris!' I am the Chris! You can't kill me! I'm instrumental in saving the universe!" I screamed. I knew how narcissistic that sounded, but I really didn't care at that point.

"Yes, we did say that!"

"That's right! So what happened? The organic CPU ran some computation and figured you're 'the Helmut' now? Is that it?" I considered the possibility that he took me here to whack me, but then it occurred to me that he didn't need to do it himself. He could send anyone to rub me out. If he controlled Enron, Circuit City, Tyrel Laboratories and any number of other companies, where could I hide? I began to feel sick, and my lips began to tremble.

"So that's it. You're going to kill me. You're going to have me disappeared."

"No, no, no!" he protested. "We don't know if you're supposed to be dead. It's just that there have been some recent indications!"

"But what about 'the Chris' you were all talking about? What happened?" My vision got blurry with tears.

"There's something wrong. You're 'the Chris,' but it might be that you're somehow attracting the Absence and not part of what seals the rift."

"Me?"

"But there are other indications that you are part of what help seals the rift. We cannot say. There's something unresolved, something unsettled."

"With what?"

He paused "With you."

"I . . . I don't understand."

"And I don't either."

"So, if you discover that I must not be roaming the earth, you're going to kill me? God, you're worse than my last job!"

"No, Chris. That won't happen."

"Well, I'm not going to do it myself. All y'all can go to hell. I didn't get sober to commit suicide. It would destroy my mom. And I know that if you think it's so goddamned important to save existence you would do anything, even murder. So, you're just going have to do it yourself. Don't be a pussy, Helmut! Don't use your goons! *You* do it!"

Yes, I reached that point where I was daring the very man who told me that I might have to die to kill me. You could say I had become unhinged.

"I won't need to do that, Chris." As he said that I could tell that Helmut was close to tears as well.

"Why won't you need to do it?"

"Because," he said as he gulped, "Because I know that if it is necessary you will do it. You would always do it, because that's who you are. You're the Chris."

So it was all about me. How narcissistic is that? Actually, at some point on the drive back to the office Helmut explained that it wasn't all about me. I was merely one of many variables. They saw a few hues that were potential candidates to be conducive to their space/time sealant device, this "analeptic quantum teleological foam." As he explained it, there were hues that were within reach, and you just sort of create the circumstances that bring you to that hue like a heading. If you can see the future results of the hues and those hues emerge from the same base hue, you can head your course accordingly.

The Stubb Foundation wasn't exactly able to see all the outcomes of all hues. Even with their order of intelligence that was a couple above our own they were still limited. But they knew a few things. There were no longer an infinite number of hues. The thing about infinity, Helmut explained months ago, is that infinity is not about numbers because numbers have no meaning in infinity, and it is impossible to wrap my mind around that. When there no longer is infinity you are dealing with something entirely different. The actual number of hues is unknown; it's beyond trying to put on paper, but there were a finite number of them now and that number was decreasing. And in some hues, the space/time Higgs Boson field was easier to work with than in others.

It just so happened that some of those candidate hues within our grasp (not the ones where Hitler won or the Cuban Missile crisis ended with a nuclear exchange, I presume) that present the best opportunities to seal the rift existed where Chris Jung would no longer be alive on October 26th.

Before I left for the day, and I did decide to take the rest of the day off what with my death becoming immanently possible, I asked Helmut one thing:

"How can I be sure you're not full of it?"

"We could be insane," he said evenly.

I shrugged my shoulders and nodded.

"The final score will be 34 to 19, the Broncos over the Falcons. Atlanta will score 13 points in the fourth quarter but will fumble on their last drive."

He was referring to the upcoming Super Bowl XXXIII. Having grown up in New Orleans I was well aware of the Saints' mortal rival the Falcons' achievement of getting into their first Super Bowl. Of course, I was supposed to root against them, but considering that Helmut just gave me such a precise prediction to prove that they were indeed on the level and not in the same credit union as the Branch Davidians, I hoped Atlanta would prevail. Helmut has never done that before, by the way, making a prediction to prove he could indeed see the future. Back when I was read into their true mission, he explained that when they were melded into the great cosmic consciousness, they could perceive themselves through several hues spanning time in an asymmetrical way, whatever that meant. But their future cast was limited similar to the way we could only see for so many miles before things are just too far away and fuzzy.

Song on my mixtape of despondency:
"Nutshell" by Alice in Chains
Visit www.michaeljuge.com on the *Here We Are Now* page to listen

I didn't return to the Stubb Foundation the following Monday or the following week. Classes started again. Before Helmut landed that bomb on me, I signed up for another array of inane classes and I switched from this *Genetics and Modalities* seminar to the *Dehistoricization of Self* because Meredith mentioned she had registered for the class at my sobriety birthday party. At the time I acted surprised, as I too was registered for the class, and soon afterwards made the switch over to that class. I showed up for the *Dehistoricization of Self* seminar and walked out ten minutes into the discussion. I just didn't see the point. I just left.

I found myself cycling a lot as I tended to do to process the reality that hit me. I went to the motor course at Emma Long Park. Part of me reckoned that if I was meant to die, this would be a likely place for me to buy the farm. It's amazing what I could do on my Kona once death was no longer as taboo.

I didn't go to the classes, but I cycled up to campus to loiter. I saw Meredith sometimes. I spied, stalked, whatever you want to call it. She spent a lot of her time at the LBJ School. She would walk to classes with her colleagues. Meredith looked so beautiful, so alive and so ready to be part of the world. I kept my distance and made sure she never saw me. While I cycled I listened to a lot of Tori Amos. I also listened to a lot of Rage Against the Machine to get my testosterone back. Both Rage and Tori got an inordinate number of songs on a mixtape I made to listen to while cycling. Spin Magazine rated it as one of the worst mixtapes ever hashed together.

The Broncos hammered the Falcons. 34 to 19, just like Helmut said. I tallied the score to find that Atlanta did score 13 points in the fourth quarter and, yes, they did fumble on their last drive allowing Denver to run out the clock, again, just like Helmut said would happen.

I was lying down in my room watching *The X-Files* episode I taped but hadn't gotten around to watching. It was the one where a crime scene photographer saw people who were about to die in black and white. Stacy knocked on the door.

"Are you 'bating?"

She could be so crude sometimes. "It's open."

She sat on the bed next to me. "So, you want to talk about it or what?"

I did. I desperately wanted to talk to her, to anyone. Normally, I would be sharing every detail of my emotions whether they wanted to hear it or not. So, why didn't I run home and call my sponsor to tell him? Why didn't I tell my best friend Stacy? Because how do you tell someone that you might have to be killed because you're part of this group that's working to save the universe. I told Stacy, Tara and Ejay about Stubb Foundation's mission to save the universe. They laughed it off and didn't take it seriously. Nobody did. Even I held a reserve of doubt. But if I told her the stakes now, would she call the cops?

As I thought about it, I didn't want her or anyone else to interfere with the Stubb Foundation's mission. I believed them. I knew they were right. *So, what do I say to Stacy?*

I paused the VHS and thought about it as we both walked onto my balcony to smoke. Maybe I had to do this. If the Stubb Foundation felt it necessary that I die, then I needed to die. I also knew I couldn't stay silent anymore.

"Stacy, there's something I need to tell you."

So, I told her everything. Stacy didn't yell at me, she didn't try to shut me down. She held my hand as I explained it. And we came up with a plan that would serve as a safeguard.

I returned to the Stubb Foundation the following morning. The Stubb Foundation members all greeted me as I came in, Sheila, Stella, Hank, Hector, Siobahn, Harry. Helmut stood by a computer console and turned around.

"So, what's the prognosis, professor? Am I tearing the universe apart or saving it?"

"We still don't know. Chris, I . . ."

I stopped him. "If you decide I need to die, then you will let me know first, and you will have me taken out in a way that looks like it was a robbery, a robbery while on the job. It cannot ever . . . *ever* look like a suicide. You hear me? And you will provide to my mother in one lump sum of five . . . no, ten million dollars within six months after my death that will go to her. That's the amount after taxes by the way. You have one of your accounts work the dollar amount needed to fulfill that. She will never want for anything. You can say I enrolled in one of your fan-fucking-tastic life insurance programs. It might be hard to believe considering you pod knockers don't even provide me health coverage, but no one will argue. And my terms are non-negotiable."

"I swear it will be done, Chris."

"Good."

"Is there anything else we can do for you?"

"Other than finding a hue within reach that doesn't involve my demise, I'm good to go. Well, I could use some assistance in my classes. I've been sort of slacking off. There are some outstanding papers. Take care of it."

"I think we can catch you up."

I showed up to class after having skipped a couple of weeks of seminars. I lied and said it was a family matter I had to attend to and the Stubb Foundation just so happened to have a doctor on retainer who was useful at times like these for writing notes about non-existent siblings in therapy at hospitals. When I walked into the *Dehistoricization of Self* seminar Meredith was noticeably surprised. I took a seat next to her. "I got lost."

After class, I walked with Meredith to her car.

"I was worried about you, Chris."

"You were?" I said with a little too much excitement. I tried to tone it down. "Oh, I mean, really?"

"Yes. You seemed so out of sorts when I saw you that first day in class. Then you walked out after a few minutes and you didn't show up for weeks. I really wanted to call, but I didn't want to intrude either."

I tried not to stare into her eyes lest I fall into them. I know, dudes across the world are gagging right now, but I swear Meredith has these deep brown eyes that just melt my resolve and any hope of being cool. Before the whole I might have to die thing happened, all I could think about that entire time off from school was Meredith: her reddish brunette hair, her soft tenor voice, the genteel womanly way she spoke, the way she walked, that orange dress that night she bought for my party. She was so demure, so beautiful, and then, well, you could say I got distracted.

"What happened?" She asked. "Are you okay?"

"Yeah. I'm fine . . . I think. It's just a stupid family thing."

Here's the funny thing about me. I'm no Stubb Foundation member privy to the probabilities of my death. Helmut tried to explain quantum mechanics to me through some guy's cat, Schrodinger—that's the name of the guy, not the cat. Schrodinger's cat is put into a metal box that is subsequently bombarded by radiation, never mind why. Now, before you open the box, in our experience we figure the cat is either dead or alive. It can be either until we open it and we determine that it is definitely dead or still alive. We presume that it was dead or alive before we opened it, but in quantum mechanics, before you open the box, the cat is both dead *and* alive. It is only at the moment when it is observed that the cat assumes a singular state; dead *or* alive. The observation itself forces a singular state of being.

I am Schrodinger's cat. Until I know what the Stubb Foundation determines, I am both dead and alive. So, I'm half dead already, right? I've seen these movies where someone already thinks he's going to die so he becomes fearless. I certainly approached mountain biking with gusto. Then why in the hell was I so damned nervous about asking Meredith out? I was a dead man walking, and yet . . . and yet . . . here I was looking down at my shoes kicking the ground trying to muster the courage to ask her out on a date.

We stood there a moment until I vocalized something to the effect of, "Hey, um, are you, you know . . . would you like to do something, like, whatever?"

Meredith translated my severely botched offer of a date. "Do you know Scott Ritter?"

"Scott? Oh, yeah, he's my boy!" I hadn't a clue who the hell Scott was. I just hoped it wasn't some guy she was dating.

"Um, yeah," she said dismissively, "anyway, Scott Ritter is the former UN weapons inspector in Iraq."

I gulped, realizing I just blundered. She continued.

"He's speaking tomorrow night over at the Student Union to discuss the reasons for his resignation."

It sounded like a perfect romantic setting, so I jumped in.

"Oh yeah, I was going to that, too! I'll pick you up!"

Meredith stuttered slightly with surprise. "Um, okay."

"And maybe we can get, you know, some coffee first, or something."

"Fair enough."

"Great. I'll pick you up at . . . um, what time was it for again?"

22

Tear gas and love is in the air

February 1999

"One, two, three, four, we don't need your fucking war!"

"The people . . . united . . . cannot be defeated!"

"Show me what democracy looks like!"

"This is what democracy looks like!"

The crowd churning from the Student Union onto Guadalupe chanted with as much cohesion and clarity as the leadership of the antiwar protest could muster. One sign showed President Bill Clinton with the word "Rapist" scrawled over his forehead. Another cardboard sign looked like it was a treatise about the nature of war itself, but the drafter apparently didn't plan ahead, because the words on the picket sign shrank like the end of the preamble text in *Star Wars* until the last few words were nothing more than .005 micro font.

"What's all this then?" I asked to no one in particular as Meredith and I walked out of the Student Union. We had just left the Scott Ritter's lecture. As expected of any former UN weapons inspector's lecture about the vagrant abuses of the inspectors and the dangers of US hegemony, it was exceedingly unerotic. But whatever, I was on a date—well, if not date—a coordinated rideshare to an event involving refreshments beforehand with Meredith. Close enough.

Meredith pushed her glasses up the bridge of her nose to keep them from falling off. She squinted, trying to figure what the rally was all about.

"Do you think it's related?"

"I don't think so, but let's check it out."

I was absolutely ecstatic. The protest? I didn't know what it was about, nor could I care less. I was ecstatic because I was on a date with Meredith Anderson. I hadn't thought about my pending demise once since I picked up her early that evening. I had my cleanest T-shirt on under an unbuttoned dress shirt under a sports coat. She meanwhile wore a gray skirt, matching tights and silver camisole under a sheer blouse.

During Scott Ritter's speech, I couldn't help but steal glances at her beautiful face, those deep brown eyes, that reddish hair and her legs. I'm a legs guy. As always, she dressed like a businesswoman. What in the hell was she doing with a guy like me sporting a ponytail with shaved sides and wearing a faded 503 Coffeehouse T-shirt?

The crowd marched, yelling slogans angrily. I recognized one of the students. He was an undergraduate, but was like ten years older than my twenty-six. He lived in the Harvest Moon Co-op, the one I got kicked out of for willful and lascivious carnivory inside a vegan household. In fact, he led the Commission of Truth and Reconciliation that had me voted out. The professional student handed out some rag called *The Daily Worker*, even though I was certain this guy hadn't worked a day in his life. But then again, the guy who had managed to be president of the University of Texas student chapter of the International Socialist Organization eight years running needed to concentrate on stuff like this and couldn't be bothered with work.

"Hey, it's Jeff, right?"

Dressed in black pajamas and Converses with a red Che T-shirt, he acknowledged me reluctantly. "It's Balou, actually."

That's right. Jeff had started referring to himself as Balou, meaning "beautiful" in Swahili or Bosque or something. I pressed on.

"What's going on? Is this about Scott Ritter?"

"Who? No, man, this is about the illegal and cowardly rape by that warmonger Clinton against the innocent peoples of Serbia."

Meredith and I leaned our heads back and said, "Oh right, that one" in unison. There was some talk on the news about the Kosovo war, and how people were upset that the president had a campaign of air missions over Serbia that had been going on for months. Some part of me felt sorry for our generation that we didn't have a comprehensive enough war worthy of getting behind or protesting. Conflicts now were brush fires hardly holding anyone's attention. It was, admittedly, a grotesque and asinine passing thought.

Then it occurred to me. "Wait, didn't the Socialists cry foul that Clinton didn't go to war *against* the Serbs when the Serbians were raping the ethnic Muslims on masse?"

"I don't know what the hell you're talking about, man!"

"No, I'm probably mistaken. It was some other Socialist group. Cool, carry on."

"Fight the power!" he cried out.

There was a stir in the crowd followed by the wail of sirens. A police officer on a megaphone squealed the intercom feedback over of the crowd.

"You are marching without a permit and are in violation of city ordinance. Break up your demonstration immediately!"

Someone yelled out, "Fuck you, pig!"

Others cheered in response, encouraging the kid. More police cars arrived. Cops in riot gear plodded up the hill, beating their batons into their gloved hands in unison. Neither Meredith nor I could pull ourselves away. This was getting good.

"Show me what democracy looks like!"

"This is what democracy looks like!" the people shouted.

Others shouted, "The people . . . united . . . shall not be defeated."

"You are hereby ordered to disperse immediately."

Someone threw a bottle, crying out some curse about the officer's mother. The bottle shattered on top of a patrol car. Someone else threw a bottle and it erupted into flames.

Song in my head: "Linger" by The Cranberries
Visit www.michaeljuge.com on the *Here We Are Now* page to listen

That's when it got interesting. The cops in the riot gear beat their batons and I heard a *thumping* sound, then saw the smoke of tear gas. Meredith and I stood in silent amazement, unable to move until the cops, lined up in a phalanx and pushed through the screaming crowd of students, the smell of tear gas and patchouli blending together in a most distinctive way. It was getting dangerous. Meredith started coughing. Fortunately, my smoking inured me from the noxious fumes. Just then a Molotov cocktail was thrown against a Starbucks across the street, followed by the sounds of heads being beaten.

"Come on, let's get out of here," I urged.

Without thinking I grabbed Meredith's hand and we ran off away from the protests. We ran hand in hand into the night, down a flight of stairs, past the iconic UT Tower and down another flight of steps until the sounds of the battle faded and the tear gas smell dissipated. We found ourselves near a fountain alone, still holding each other's hands. I had originally taken it without thinking. Now, I wished never to let go.

She giggled. "Ho . . . ly . . . shit!"

Sirens screamed and out in the distance someone with an amp busted out some Rage Against the Machine to encourage the protestors. I knew the song to be "Township Rebellion." I had played it a lot this past month . . . that along with Tori Amos.

As I caught my breath, I looked into her eyes. I felt my heart racing, and my knees felt weak. She was still holding my hand.

It was a moment in time, a perfect moment. We looked into each other's eyes, and for a split second I understood what Helmut meant when he said that in infinity numbers mean nothing. In this moment, time meant nothing except that I never wanted this moment to end. This moment was its own hue independent from everything that came before it and that would follow. Maybe it was something fundamentally more. Every moment built up to this singular hegemonic moment and every moment thereafter would be contextualized by it.

"So . . . here we are now," she said. She looked at me expectantly.

I repeated what she said to myself. And then I realized, if only for that moment, that I didn't need to know what would happen to me. I didn't need to know whether I would live or not, what I would do with my life if I should live. I need not plan out my path like I thought I was supposed to. This was the only moment for me that counted. Here . . . now. *Yes. Here we are now.*

She wrapped her hands around mine.

I couldn't just make the move, though. Oh, no. Why? Because I'm an idiot that way.

"Wow, I have to say, this is a good way to spend a Sunday evening," I added as though I needed to add anything.

She moved closer. "Yes. It makes missing *The X-Files* worth it."

"You . . . you like the *X-Files, too?*"

"I *love* the *X-Files*," she professed sincerely.

With Zack de la Rocha howling in the background "Fight the war, fuck the norm" and the wail of sirens bouncing off the building walls, I wrapped my arm around her waist and pressed myself close to her. It was time to take a chance. Meredith pulled my face to hers and we kissed. Somewhere nearby, someone released a volley of fireworks.

23

Not just for the nookie

Spring 1999

The next three months were about moments. I showed Meredith the Austin I had come to know. All those years of driving throughout the Hill Country and cycling around town paid off. We hiked Enchanted Rock, I took her all over the Greenbelt to all these secluded spots that nobody knew about. Meredith took me to galleries and to random historical sites that everyone had forgotten. I introduced her to coffeehouses, she introduced me to Ethiopian cuisine. I introduced her to the varieties of coffee and she introduced me to Fruitopia. I introduced her to *South Park* while she introduced me to Book People. Did you know that before we started dating, Meredith would go to Book People on Friday nights not to meet guys, but just to look at *books*? I know, right? I took her away from all of that.

Maybe it was the realization that my existence was finite no matter the date of my expiration. All I knew was that that spring I experienced a series of moments where I was truly present. It's hard to explain. I was super-saturated into the moment with Meredith as though I knew that this moment happened once and was unique. Some moments were enlightening, some touching, some randy. Others weren't particularly earth shattering or anything, and yet . . . I don't know . . . they just stood out for some reason.

Meredith and I stayed low key about dating in the beginning. We didn't tell anyone in the Anthropology Department for weeks. I don't know why, really. I guess Meredith was a really cautious type. She was definitely a deeply private person. Unlike myself, Meredith didn't dump her emotions on the first person willing to hear them. She was reserved, dignified, and she was neither easily impressed (as I learned early on) nor was she easily swayed by emotionalism. In many ways we were the yin and yang, at least to the outward observer we were. She also was very cautious about any commitments. I had to convince her that I had no intention of ensnaring her into a relationship that she wasn't comfortable with.

"Look, let's just have fun and see how things go," she said.

I had learned from the past that being clingy is not sexy for some reason. So, I had to restrain myself. I had to just accept the volatility of this undefined and passionate thing between us.

Song on the stereo:
"Here The Story Ends" by The Sundays
Visit www.michaeljuge.com on the *Here We Are Now* page to listen

Sometimes she would walk out from an anthropology class and pull me into an empty classroom to make out before anyone discovered us. She would then shoo me away, fix her hair and act as if we were mere acquaintances as we passed each other by in the quad. Sometimes she and I would walk together around campus holding hands. She would suddenly rip her hand from me when someone we recognized came by. Normally, I would be offended, but then she would make up for it by being really affectionate later. Still, I didn't know if she was ashamed to be with me, if she was enjoying the idea of a secret romance or if she really was being adamant in maintaining the standard that we weren't an "item."

So, it's no wonder why I remember the first time we arrived to an anthropology function as a couple so well. It wasn't an anthropology function really. Gary was hosting a party, and it included students from anthropology along with Middle Eastern studies, cultural studies, economics and library sciences. I picked up Meredith at her place, and she was wearing this enticing perfume. As we drove over to Gary's off of Far West Boulevard, I turned on the stereo. I didn't realize what I had in the tape deck. It was The Sundays.

"Oh, sorry. It's Cliff's," I said lying through my teeth. If I had been one of Cliff's tapes it would be something like P.O.D. or Korn.

"It's fine. I love this song!"

"Oh, okay. I usually listen to Nine Inch Nails by the way." I don't know why, but I was so embarrassed. I guess I wished I had something more masculine on like Limp Bizkit. Hell, even R.E.M. was would be more manly.

"No, really, you have no idea how much I love this song," she insisted.

"Really?"

"Oh, yes. I remember when this song came out. I grew up a half-hour outside Madison and I was dating a guy who went to the University of Wisconsin."

I did the math in my head. She was a year younger than me, so . . . "Wait. When this song came out? That was in 1990. We were both still in high school."

"That's right."

"But you just said you were dating a guy in college." Meredith gave me a look and then I nodded knowingly. Meredith wasn't the first girl I heard of in high school dating college boys. Hell, most of my girl friends dated boys in college when we were mere sophomores in high school, and I was there to pick up the emotional pieces every time. It was part of my responsibility given my super powers to befriend pretty girls with remarkable platonic regularity.

"It was a great time. He introduced to this radio station on campus, which in turn introduced me to a whole new world of music I'd never heard before. That song sort of encapsulated that time in my life."

Meredith smiled. "That was when I became energized to get involved in the world. I became geo-politically aware that semester. I wanted us to spend our resources on improving the lives of people in our own country instead of expending resources and lives to protect our oil from Saddam."

She smirked. "Sounds pretty foolish, doesn't it?"

I turned to face her. "No, not at all. I mean, a little naïve maybe, but that was high school. Who wasn't a little idealistic then?"

I could see little high school Meredith with her raven hair holding a protest sign yelling with her Wisconsin accent she probably worked hard to erase in the years since, "No blood for oil" or volunteering at soup kitchens.

As we drove over to pick up some wine from Central Market we both started humming along and singing the refrain. Meredith then started rifling through my cassette case. I had failed to vet it before picking her up, a crucial error. You could tell a lot by the music one listened to. The cassette case in *Value Menus* contained some Rage and Nine Inch Nails along with some obscure stuff Gary lent me to include Death Cab For Cutie and My Bloody Valentine. But primarily I was stuck in my parents' generation with The Doors, The Animals and Pink Floyd. I could be seen as someone stuck in the past with a lack of imagination and daring. That would not be good.

But as soon as the Sundays ended, she ejected the cassette and put in Velvet Underground. We got caught in a snarl on Mopac as "All Tomorrow's Parties" fade in. She took my hand and we sat in traffic in silence listening.

When we walked into Gary's house, Meredith didn't let go of my hand. I hadn't expected that. I made a point to respect her commitment to keeping our relationship a secret. Her holding my hand in front of the Anthropology Department caused quite a stir. Heather and Andre, now a couple, stared in amazement, Margaret gave the head nod of approval as she knew Meredith to be a good bird. The others just stood there trying to make sense of us. The two of us together, it just seemed so odd. Gary welcomed us and we joined his friends Mindy, Albert and others. There was also the obligatory aging hippie per city ordinance. I swore I'd seen this particular hippie before. Stacy came over as well. I found this odd, because she didn't mention anything to me about coming to the party. What was she doing here? And then I noticed she and Gary greeting each other with a kiss. *Ah ha.* Spring is in the air, indeed. The two of them worked on something together. Gary was on the sound system while Stacy connected his PC to the master control board.

"Now, what in the world do you think those two are up to?" I asked Meredith.

"I think Stacy's using the computer to control the music."

Meredith was far more erudite in computers than I. My grandmother was, as well, so that wasn't really saying much.

"How's that?" I asked.

"I'm not sure. I read something in Fast Company how mp3s are beginning to replace CDs."

"What's an mp3?"

Just as Meredith was about to explain the next great media format that would render my already obsolete cassettes and my growing CD collection completely obsolete, we heard the start of "Smells Like Teen Spirit."

All Gen Xers swore by Nirvana. It didn't matter your political leanings, your demographic or your general taste in music. Nirvana was our generation's Beatles. It altered the musical and cultural landscape with that one song cleansing the mainstream malaise of '80s hair bands. Oddly enough, most Gen Xers still didn't know the lyrics to our generation's anthem, but we knew that whatever Kurt Cobain was mumbling it was important and that he voiced our sense of untethered angst. An entire genre followed right behind that song to storm the beaches of pop culture. The opening strum of "Smells Like Teen Spirit" was an ominous wail to the likes of Poison and Motley Crue, portending that their days of wanton objectification and soulless corporate rock were over. That is what I thought at the time, anyway. What I never saw coming was how grunge and the Gen X counter culture in general would be acculturated and appropriated so thoroughly by the same corporate machine that brought you Poison and Motley Crue. But I digress.

So, we heard the signature start to "Smells Like Teen Spirit," with the guitar riff, but when Kurt Cobain was supposed to sing "Load up on guns, bring your friends," the craziest thing since my learning that the universe could be devoured into the Absence happened. Rick Astley, that '80s one-hit wonder, started singing his song "Never Gonna Give You Up." My mind nearly exploded right then and there.

Everyone stopped doing whatever it was they were doing to listen to this most impossible—I don't know what you call it, a "mash up," between Nirvana and Rick Astley. When we realized what Gary had done we all cheered raucously and moshed to Rick Astley. And here's the weird thing: Those two songs merged perfectly together. This mash up between the two songs was seamless to the point that I began to wonder if Nirvana had stolen their riffs from Rick Astley. Whatever the case, it was brilliant. I was convinced that Gary Hughes was a freaking genius.

During that spring I went to Meredith's symposiums on water policy in the Arab world, coordination of NGOs through the Internet and eCommerce in economically distressed urban areas in the US. I brought the Lord of the Flies crew for moral support and to prevent a Sheldon-like troll from attempting to knock her work.

Meredith tutored me through the semester's work. She had drafted an extensive glossary over past two years to decrypt post-structuralism and re-encrypt from English back to post-modernism for papers. She had her own work to attend to, yet she took the time out for me. Eventually, I was able to hold my own in class.

Meredith didn't own a TV, which is totally savage. She got into *The X-Files* by watching it at the apartment lobby while doing her laundry. She lived in one of the new university ghettos off of Riverside east of the I-35. So, when we started dating, I was only too happy to have her come over to the Travis Heights house Sunday evenings to watch *X-Files*. I never cared for Sundays. Ever since I was a kid, Sunday was a purgatory of waiting for the inevitable coming of Monday. And now Sunday evening meant five more days until Meredith and I could be together as a couple again. The work week was just too busy for both of us: she with her dual program in anthropology and public affairs and me with school and the Stubb Foundation. *The X-Files* was a way to convince Meredith to come over one last time before our weekly five-day hiatus.

Those moments sometimes lasted seconds, sometimes minutes, sometimes hours, and I wanted to stay there. But as Axl Rose so famously said, "nothing lasts forever." Spring semester ended and Meredith headed to New York City to do a summer internship at the UN. She would be gone for the next three months.

I had known for some time that Meredith was going to head off to New York City for the summer. I tried not to dwell on it and to just enjoy the springtime romance. Meredith made no secret that she was hesitant about commitments, so I had to play it cool. It wasn't something I was particularly skilled at doing, but I managed to part ways with dignity, though it was really unceremonious rushing her to the airport. I had forgotten that the Robert Mueller airport had just closed the week before and replaced by the new Austin Bergstrom International airport twenty minutes away. Fortunately, I was a courier and knew the secret wormhole of the 183. We had a rushed goodbye at the departure lane rather than a proper goodbye at the gate (yes, you could accompany someone to the gate back then). After dropping her off, I drove back home alone playing "All Tomorrow's Parties."

24

Moby Summer

Summer 1999

I had become accustomed to weird happenings inside the Stubb Foundation. They were working on all kinds of projects that made absolutely no sense. Just the week before, I saw Hank and Shelly listening to various songs repeatedly. Among them, they played a bar of Neil Diamond's "Song Sung Blue," playing it forwards and backwards in super slow mode. By the time I went to get lunch, I was convinced that Neil Diamond was sending nihilistic messages such as, "goes, goes to the abyss."

This morning I walked in sulking. As I put my bike away, I saw half of the Stubb Foundation members hunched over a table testing the absorbent strength of various tampons. I just shook my head. I couldn't believe these guys could convince me to die.

Helmut emerged from the upper level where I learned the organic CPU was housed.

"Chris, I'm going to need you to take a trip."

I raised my eyebrows. "Really, a trip like somewhere not in Austin?"

"Yes, I need you to fly up to New York to deliver some papers to . . ."

I didn't hear what he said from there because I was jumping up and down for joy.

". . . and since it will be a Friday, you can stay the weekend. But I need you to be in DC that Monday morning to meet with the congressman."

What? I'm supposed to meet with some congressman? Wouldn't he be better for such things?

Whatever the reason for Helmut sending me, I was given a reprieve from what had to be the inevitable goodbye from Meredith as opposed to last week. This was my chance to say goodbye nice and proper. Yes, I know, we were going to be apart for only three months. In theory, we could continue where we left off after she returned. There are a few key problems with such an optimistic projection:

- First, the sum total of time we had been dating was roughly three months.
- Second, Helmut might require me to shove off this mortal coil before the end of summer.
- Third, and this is the most important qualification, Meredith was way out of my league. I considered our whole fling this spring to be charitable work on her part to the less advantaged chubsters like myself. Meredith was going to be away in New York City for three months surrounded by successful and ambitious men. So, this trip would be my chance to say goodbye. I could then concentrate on the fate of my life and the universe.

I was nervous as I stood inside the super shuttle making its way from LaGuardia to Manhattan. How would this go? I desperately wanted to see Meredith again, but what if I screwed the pooch? I mean, the last time she saw me we were in a rush to make it to the airport, but at least that parting was on a positive note. What if she forgot I was coming in today? What if that week apart afforded her enough time to come to her senses? What if this was a bad idea? I couldn't believe it, but I was now beginning to reconsider visiting Meredith. And then I slapped myself, I literally slapped myself, inside the cabin of the super shuttle, as if to say, "Pull yourself together, damn it!" No one on the super shuttle paid any attention.

I staggered off the super shuttle with my duffle and messenger bag in tow outside the gates of Columbia University's campus. It's where they were housing the UN interns for the summer. I hoped I had gotten the instructions right. A gaggle of people walked past, and then I saw her sitting on the low set stonewall. Meredith Anderson saw me and smiled. She was wearing the orange dress she bought for my party back in December. That was a wonderful sign.

Song heard throughout the city: "Porcelain" by Moby
Visit www.michaeljuge.com on the *Here We Are Now* page to listen

Before I could forget the official reason for my visit, I grabbed Meredith and we took a taxi to deliver the documents from the Stubb Foundation to Worldcom, where I received hearty handshakes from these businessmen. I don't know what it was I handed them, but after signing them and returning them back to me, they took Meredith and me out to lunch at one of the best steakhouses and Meredith got girl drink drunk. They also gave us tickets to see something called "De La Guarda."

Throughout that weekend, Meredith and I heard Moby being played wherever we went. After seeing *De La Guarda* Meredith and I walked around the East Village and we heard Moby being played in no less than five bars we passed. After hearing it in restaurants, bars, at street fairs and even outside a federal courthouse we each bought the bootleg copy of Moby's CD *Play*, and played it repeatedly in her dorm room late into the evening. New York City was humming with songs like "Honey" and "South Side." *Play* was ever-present as if it was the soundtrack to our weekend together.

It was the night before I was to depart. Meredith and I huddled together in the twin bed inside the dorm room listening to . . . yeah, Moby again. We were both dozing off but trying to stay awake so that we could keep the discussion going, pushing the inevitable march of the minutes.

"Chris," she whispered. "Do you think Krycek is secretly working to resist the Syndicate?"

I forgot to mention that a lot of our discussions veered into *The X-Files* and Meredith had a thing for the bad boy character.

"Meh, I think he's for himself."

We uttered a few more theories about the season finale until there was a silence. The CD was playing "Porcelain," and I was nearly asleep. I felt Meredith's warmth next to mine and caressed her hair. Moments. Just moments.

"Meredith," I whispered softly, "I love you."

I jumped out of my skin realizing what I had just done. My eyes shot a look. I was awaiting the God awful, "Oh, that's sweet." *Chris, what did you do, What. Did. You. Do?*

There was no response. I felt the rhythmic pattern of her breathing indicating that she had fallen asleep. *Phew.* That was a close one.

The following evening we visited my older brother Jack. I didn't tell you about him? Jack looked like me except three years older and roughly twenty pounds lighter both in muscle and fat. Jack took us to some restaurant in Alphabet City where we had ravioli with squid ink. While swallowing down squid ink ravioli, I asked Jack what his company subVerse Engineering did.

"We're online marketing research optimization consultants."

Now, that's enough to shut me up. I heard those words and I didn't want to look dumb, so I replied, "Oh, neat."

Meredith, on the other hand, was not fazed by the lingo at all. "What is your business model?" she asked innocently.

Jack gave her a confused look. "How do you make money," she rephrased.

Jack stuttered and mumbled something to the effect that, "It's complicated."

"It shouldn't be. Are you a service provider? What is your product line?"

For the first time in my life, I saw Jack squirm. Finally he said, "Well, it's seed money for now, really."

I don't know, but something about that exchange made me fall for her harder. Afterwards, Jack invited us to a party at subVerse Engineering, as it was going to go public on Monday. Everyone at subVerse was going to be rich. Jack brought us over to the top of a brownstone in the Bowery for the IPO party.

Places like the Bowery and the Lower Eastside always conjured the image of the seediest sections of Gotham where you were guaranteed to get mugged by a multi-ethnic gang wearing some kind of uniform or at least wearing masks, or hoods with striped shirts. The turn of the century architecture, film noir fog and grime along with the constant smell of dog urine and pigeon droppings permeating the city lent credence to that impression. Upon arriving, I was somewhat disappointed to find the Bowery was now populated by a bunch of upwardly mobile Gen Xers whose upbringing in places like Connecticut and suburbs of New Jersey made me and Jack seem urban in comparison with our NOLA credentials.

I read something about this "gentrification" thing in one of Meredith's magazines: Harpers, Wired or The Atlantic—I forget which one. She subscribed to magazines that used words like "insouciant." This gentrification was a thing in places like New York City, Washington, DC, Baltimore, even Pittsburgh. It was a foreign concept to me. New Orleans didn't have gentrification. It had white flight. You wanted gritty realism? You don't need to spend $2,000 a month for a tiny apartment in the Bowery or Williamsburg, Brooklyn. Come to New Orleans. We have old dilapidated buildings all over the place. No jobs, but we have old buildings. Austin? It's hard to say Austin was gentrifying when it never had been poor, urban, or blighted in the first place. No, Austin was expanding, not gentrifying.

After dropping off my duffle and messenger bag in Jack's office, Meredith and I walked up the seven stories to the roof of the building. Jack introduced me to his colleagues. They were remarkably similar to Stacy's coworkers at Rapture and CynerDygm along with the employees at countless startups throughout Austin like iSoar, Tantric Dynamics or Ethereal. subVerse had an impressive spread outside. We really didn't need to get dinner beforehand.

The roof was packed with people. Part of me wished I hadn't taken my brother's invitation. These were my final hours with Meredith. I should have spent them with her alone. Chemical Brothers was playing in the background. Jack gestured for us to come over. As we made our way through, I overheard people's conversations.

"I think *The Matrix* will redefine how movies are made. No more of the banal shit. For now on, we'll demand depth with our action movies!"

"IPO, man! This is it! I'm gonna retire and move to Alaska and own an apple orchard."

"Do apples grow in Alaska?"

"I'm telling you, this new economy is going to usher in a whole new age of unprecedented prosperity. In ten years, the world will have been democratized through the Internet, war will become passé."

"Oh, totally! It's a paradigm shift of epic proportions. I predict in ten years we won't even recognize this place."

"So, I heard Apple is working on a portable mp3 player."

"Why would someone want that?"

"No moving parts in an mp3!"

"Yeah, but no CD cover to add to your collection. No one will see what you own."

We met up with Jack, who was talking to a somewhat nerdy-looking guy with a shaved head and glasses, which according to my observation was trendy in New York City. I expect it would hit Austin in a couple of months, and the rest of the country would follow in a year or so.

"Chris, I'd like you to meet a good friend of mine. Moby, this is my brother Chris and his girlfriend, Meredith."

"Hi guys, pleased to meet you."

I think both of our jaws dropped roughly in the same instant. I shook his hand and told Moby he was a musical genius. Moby seemed to be really cool about my being so star struck. Fortunately, I happened to have the bootlegged CD in my messenger bag along with a pirated copy of *Fight Club*. God, I love Chinatown. Moby signed the cover and I don't think he knew it was pirated. Either that or he didn't care.

Normally, a cameo appearance by the likes of Moby would be enough to take all of my attention. But as exciting as that was, I was distracted as the minutes passed. I calculated how long it would take to get to Penn Station from the Bowery and knew that the time had come. It was time for me to leave.

I turned to Meredith who nodded somberly. "I'll walk you downstairs."

We left the party just as a police helicopter flew overhead and waited for a taxicab. I hoped it would take awhile for one to arrive. I tried to tell myself this was just a springtime romance. Getting her to hold my hand in public was an accomplishment in itself. The moment had finally come for us to part as a taxicab approached. As it came to a stop, we kissed one last time. Moments, fleeting moments. I wanted to stay in the moment forever. I wanted to hold the taste of her lips and the smell of her perfume in my senses.

"Um, I'll email you"

"I look forward to it. Take care."

"And you, too."

As the taxi cruised up to Penn Station, I pulled out my Discman from my duffle bag and played the signed pirated copy of Moby's *Play*. The song was "Porcelain."

25

Breakfast tacos and oblivion

June 1999

On a good day, Washington DC is a letdown compared to New York City. That's not even accounting for leaving your greatest love behind for a congressional meet and greet. I staggered out of Union Station to take a taxi to Arlington. It was a damned good thing the Stubb Foundation was paying, because they had a racket in DC with cabs. Where taxi services in the first world charged by time and mileage, DC taxis charged by zone. My courier instincts told me the entire drive from Union Station in Washington DC across the Potomac to the Rosslyn neighborhood of Arlington, Virginia was no more than six miles, but we crossed something like eight zones. I think I helped the taxi driver pay for his kids' college with that fare.

Helmut was explicit that I was to meet with U.S. Rep. Gus Grady at his private residence in Rosslyn, and not at his office. You might remember Congressman Bill "Gus" Grady from such C-Span coverage as the Congressional Ethics Committee hearings where he was censured. He would later be indicted for criminal misuse of campaign funds for personal gain. To the common liberal, he was a craven hypocrite talking about his special relationship with Jesus while profiteering on the side. To the common conservative, he was a victim of the liberal media. Without context, I could totally see where Grady was seen as kind of an asshole. He called Clinton a Communist and made these horrible jokes about gays and lesbians. If he were running in my district, I wouldn't have voted for him.

Whereas the District itself was populated by majestic, albeit cold, stone and mortar office buildings from the turn of the century, the Rosslyn neighborhood of Arlington at the turn of the millennium was still blighted with a sea of brown brick buildings from the 1970s. It was perhaps the ugliest, most uninspiring downtown. The taxi drove up a hill and dropped me off at an apartment building, the private residence of Congressman Grady, where I was let in.

I'd seen Grady on TV a couple of times. He represented one of the districts in one of the wealthiest outer suburbs of Houston. He answered the door wearing a jogging outfit. Even though I was taller, he seemed imposing. He let me in and made me breakfast as he was making himself some eggs. I felt a little awkward being so casually dressed around a congressman, with my sweat-stained Quack's Coffeehouse T-shirt. Even in his jogging outfit, Grady appeared to be refined.

"You have the papers from Worldcom?" he asked as he passed me a plate of homemade breakfast tacos. It's a Texas thing.

I reached into my messenger bag and handed him the documents the ecstatic executives at Worldcom signed and handed over to me.

We sat quietly while Grady read through the documents. He signed some papers, closed the file and handed it back to me.

"I believe you have a message for me," he said gruffly.

Helmut briefed me on what to say to Gus and how to react given likely responses Gus would give. Though I wasn't exactly sure, I think I got the Gestalt of what the message and potential responses were all about. I sighed and nervously relayed the message.

"Yes. Helmut said that the funds will have to be funneled through your campaign."

"Is he sure? Couldn't the funds go through a super PAC instead? That would exculpate me from any improprieties."

"Sorry," I said weakly. "Helmut anticipated that, and he said that it was not to be. The funds *must* be carried through your campaign."

He slammed his fist on the table. "Damn it! This could land me in jail! Does he know that? And for what? That the universe *might* implode into nothing? What difference does it make where the funds come from?"

Apparently, Congressman Grady had been read onto the fate of the universe. He wasn't just some tool that Helmut used; he was invested in this.

"He told you about the nothing? We call it the Absence now, by the way."

He snorted. "Yeah. What a wonderful gift your boss gave me, the knowledge that the universe will devoured by this *Absence* as you call it created by our ingrate descendants several million years from now. They're probably a bunch of atheists and commie liberals, I bet."

"Is the government aware?"

"What? Are you on crack, son? Of course they aren't. You think I would be concerned about getting indicted for misappropriation of funds from that Funky Freiburger guy if this were sanctioned by powers that be? No, it's just me, thee and our friends back in Austin."

I didn't know that Alfi Funky Freiburger, the very same benefactor who had gotten me into graduate school, was involved in the scheme to save the universe through some misappropriation of campaign funds. What an intricate tapestry this universe was. Gus took my plate and his and brought them to the sink.

"And now he wants me to sacrifice my career on this calculation of theirs to move into the right timeline. What a joke."

"I can understand your apprehension."

"Can you? Really? What was it for you that got you on board with them? Did you learn your favorite coffeehouse might have to go out of business?" he gestured at my shirt.

"Not exactly," I said acidly, and I suddenly felt perturbed by his complaining. "I've got bigger problems than losing a chairmanship on the Y2K Commission or even an indictment. I'm probably going to have to give up my life, *sir*, so spare me your whining!"

I didn't realize just how upset I was over this until just this moment. "I'm at the prime of my life! I have a future! Hell, I've been *dieting* for God's sake! And there's every possibility that my life will have to end in order to put us into the right hue."

Gus looked at me quizzically at first, and I realized "hue" was my word, which the Stubb Foundation appropriated just like "the Absence," but he understood in the end. His own anger had evaporated.

"I'm sorry to hear that, son. I really am. But how does my demise help?"

I felt a surge of confidence. I had the upper hand after all. I was the one who had to make the greater sacrifice. It was then I realized why Helmut sent me. I could provide the congressman an example of someone being asked to sacrifice his own life, which trumped a career. In the time I spent with Meredith, I had learned how to ask the right questions. It was time to use what I learned from her.

"Do you think Helmut is wrong?"

"He has no evidence that this will happen."

I took a moment to think, another Meredith move. "But you know he's right, don't you?"

He stood silent and I went proceeded. "It seems to me that whether there's proof or not, you know he's telling you the truth." I let the silence settle a little longer against my own instincts, but again, it was a Meredith skill I was aping.

"Maybe it would be better to let the universe collapse," he muttered, somewhat like a petulant teenager would. I held a trump card Helmut gave me for this moment, and for a wonder, my timing was excellent.

"Then you would never see your granddaughter."

"What granddaughter. I don't . . ." He stopped himself. He eyes registered shock.

"Katy is pregnant, congressman. She's only a few weeks along and she's frightened. She doesn't want her parents to find out, as it would embarrass the family."

Gus slumped into his chair. Helmut told me to tell him about his daughter, who was a sophomore in college.

"My God . . . she's . . . it's going to be a girl?" I could tell that despite the blow upon hearing his daughter hadn't abided by the abstinence pledge, he was also happy to hear about a granddaughter.

"There won't be any granddaughter, not if you don't do your part. But go ahead. Be a chicken and let all existence dissolve into oblivion and never see your daughter become a mom. And I'm sure God will be quite pleased by that last act of cowardice of yours."

I wish I had a mic to drop, because I just nailed it with the God part. That was mine, by the way.

Tears were streaming down Gus' face. We sat at the table for a minute or so. Slowly, he nodded.

"Of course, I'll do it. And tell Helmut the lab will be ready on time and cleared of all personnel. Also tell him that I will have the airspace cleared in the immediate vicinity. I have some strings I can pull at the FAA."

I felt enormously relieved. Saving the universe was still on, and I somehow in some uncharacteristically sophisticated move convinced a congressman to fall on his sword.

"I'm glad to hear it. I know we will all be grateful."

"Hey," he stopped me. "I hope it won't be necessary about you, you know, having to die."

"Me too." As I walked out, I turned around. "Katy is scared, sir. She is terrified about you finding out."

"I'm taking the next flight home. She's my girl. I will always be proud of her," he said.

I waved goodbye and headed back down, satisfied that I had a Scott Bakula *Quantum Leap* moment reuniting families and convincing people to do the right thing. It made leaving Meredith a little more tolerable.

26

Slutty poetry and the Jell-0 mold that is existence

Summer 1999

I took a taxi directly from Austin Bergstrom Airport to work to pick up *Value Menus*. Helmut said he needed it for some reason. On the way over, the taxi driver who arrived from Jamaica about nine months ago complained how annoying all the newcomers to Austin were, especially the damned Californians, and lamented how the city was getting all commercial. When the taxi pulled up to the Stubb Foundation, I found that Helmut had taken the liberty of pimping my ride. He had replaced the old cassette stereo and speakers on *Values Menus* with a top-of-the-line sound system to include sub woofers and a Pioneer CD changer. I was almost disappointed not to see hydraulics, neon lights or art glass in the back with gothic letters saying "Value Menus."

I walked in and pointed to my pickup outside. "Part of saving the universe?"

"Yep," Helmut replied. "Very good job, by the way. I knew you could do it. You have the paperwork he signed?"

"Yeah, right here." As I dug into my messenger bag, I was struck by another bout of déjà vu. I shook my head. "Man this is getting weird."

Helmut nodded. "You're sensing it."

"What?"

"The déjà vu. You're experiencing right now, aren't you?"

I paused. "Yes I am as a matter of fact. How . . ." I stopped myself. They already were able to glean a lot of my memories. It stood to reason then they could figure when I was having a short-term memory fart. But then I realized something. Maybe the spate of déjà vu I had been experiencing was telling of something significant.

"Helmut, the déjà vu, it means something to you."

"Yes. When you are having déjà vu, you're experiencing the merger of two or more hues into a single hue."

"Whoa. So, you're experiencing it, too?"

"As we experience reality within a variety of close proximity hues, we experience something similar to déjà vu as a constant. But . . ." he paused, "we have been sensing a more severe form of it. And you, well, it's normal that people will experience a bout every now and then. Hues merge and splinter all the time."

"But I've been experiencing it a lot lately," I said. "The hues are collapsing more rapidly, aren't they?"

Helmut nodded grimly. He then put a hand on my shoulder. "Let's get to work, shall we? There's a lot we need to get finalized before the 26th."

I tried to convince myself that it was best to leave the relationship on a high note. Meredith and I had a proper movie-style goodbye with me leaving in a taxi on a foggy New York City street in the middle of the night. We had a perfect last weekend together. We even met Moby! I wasn't one of the brains at the Stubb Foundation, so I couldn't say for certain what would happen. But if I were a betting man, I wouldn't put stock that Meredith would maintain interest in some goof who was not in her daily presence while a bunch of high-powered guys were lying in wait. Logic would dictate that I should save myself from an epic heartbreak and try to forget about Meredith. But logic and I didn't get on too well. I was going to ride this love train until it barreled down into the ravine in flames.

Meredith and I talked on the phone a lot and I discovered something new: Hotmail. I wrote these letters late at night and wanted to send them immediately, but I was stuck with a UT email account and Stacy's

PC didn't have the software license to connect to the UT network. I didn't want to drive to the Stubb Foundation and walk in on them unannounced.

And then Stacy suggest to me one day, "Chris, just get Hotmail. It's a free email account you access from the Internet."

"Any Internet?" I still wasn't well-versed on what this Internet was. You ever heard the story of the guy who called customer service and asked, "Is this the Internet?" Yeah.

"Um, yeah. It's all the Internet."

"You said it's free email?"

"Uh huh."

I couldn't understand why a company would give away free email accounts. Didn't they have to store emails on a server somewhere? I mean, it had to go *somewhere*, right? What was in it for them? Well, free was in my price range. So, I started emailing Meredith.

I would wait until Stacy and Ejay were off the phone and then I would dial in. I wrote my letter on Word, checked for spelling and grammar, then pasted it onto this Hotmail email and hit send. I was like a computer guy now! I soon discovered that Meredith would be on the other end of the Internet while I was on, and she would respond to an email I just sent. It was awesome! We would interact live through this medium. It was better than talking on the phone with the long awkward silences—you know how much I hate awkward silences. The email exchanges weren't quite instant messaging, that would be a bridge too far for me back then, but this form of communication gave me time to collect my thoughts and respond in a coherent and articulate way, much more so than over the phone.

Meredith and I chatted over email nightly. Every once in awhile, the connection was severed when someone would call our phone and disconnect the modem's link. I would then have to redial and wait for the handshake as I learned it was called. I got pretty savvy after awhile. I started sending some poetic verses. Tara lent me her collection of obscure erotic poets and I plagiarized the hell out of them. It was a desperate act, but I was a desperate boy in love, so sue me. The emails got pretty steamy, especially when the coffee kicked in.

I had a little time on my hands one evening and our house had these left over Jell-O packets from filling a kiddie pool full of Jell-O for the 4th of July party. No need to get into details why we would do such a thing. Suffice it to say, nobody was seriously injured. Party tip: If you are inclined to throw a Jell-O pool party, know that it's cheaper to buy 10 pound bags of unflavored gelatin and mix in food coloring separately rather than buying hundreds of pouches of store-brand flavored Jell-O. Anywho, I was up late and I thought about how Helmut liked my quivering multi-colored Jell-O mold concept for existence. Remember that?

- All space and time is like multicolored Jell-O that quivers, because not everything is static.
- The colors or hues represent the myriad (though no longer infinite) realities
- Just as white light is made up of several hues, the hues share the same space/time and they borrow from each other like a timeshare.

So, I decided I should make such a Jell-O mold out of the leftover quarter-pound of clear gelatin powder. I poured the clear gelatin mixture into a Bundt cake pan and waited to add the food coloring until it was about to solidify. The food coloring hues ejaculated across a finite length of time as realities often do. Blue, yellow, red and green blobs were interspersed sporadically in the cake mold, sometimes merging to form different colors. The colors by and large kept to themselves, creating a multi-colored though still mostly clear Jell-O mold. But then I realized a problem with my representational model. Just as the food coloring didn't spread evenly throughout the mixture, then what was I saying? Were certain hues not represented throughout all of space? That couldn't be. In this Bundt cake-shaped universe, how is time distinguished from space?

With no answer to that, I took a picture anyway just to finish off the roll so I could get the photos of our sticky 4th of July celebration developed. After I got the pictures developed, I brought the photo of the Jell-O mold over to the Stubb Foundation.

Helmut looked at it and said, "Exactly!"

"But no, I didn't distinguish between time and space in the Bundt cake mold."

He looked at me quizzically. I explained that I thought that time should be represented in layers either from top to bottom or snaking around the Bundt cake in a circular pattern, but all the hues should cover all of space regardless of the length of time it exists. He shook his head vigorously. "No, existence is not a layer cake, Chris."

"Yeah, but I was trying to show how a hue might only exist for a certain length of time and then be subsumed again, but here it looks like the hue doesn't cover the entire space of the universe just as it doesn't cover all of time."

"Why would it?"

I gestured wildly. "Because . . . you know, a reality would have to cover the entire space at a given time, right?"

He grinned.

I was getting nervous. I don't know why, but I felt things were unraveling. So I pressed on with my argument. "Like, let's say this hue we're in at the moment lasts only an hour. Fine. But it has to cover all of space, because otherwise, you could have a hue where, I don't know, west of Congress Avenue the Soviets won the Cold War while east of Congress Avenue, the US did. That can't be, because there would be a contradiction."

"No it wouldn't."

"Yes it would! I'd walk from the west side of the street to the east side and I would be in a totally different hue. That's space I'm crossing, not time."

He smiled. "You don't see it, do you? You still think that there is a real difference between space and time."

"But there is, isn't there?"

"The Jell-O of space/time is exactly that. It's one thing." He paused. "Are you still with me?"

"Yes."

"Oh . . . good! Usually, this is where you black out."

But I didn't black out. I was still with him, trying to understand. I guess this was a good sign that I was still in the conversation. I tried to absorb the idea that a hue, a reality, could exist within a confined amount of space as well as limited length of time. He explained that east of Congress could be in a hue where the whole Monica Lewinsky scandal never broke, while west of Congress nobody can look at cigars the same way again.

"Ahh, but when I cross the street, I would know! I would see the historical changes going from one hue to another."

"Really? You haven't noticed this whole time you've been working for us or even while we were talking."

If you didn't catch that, Helmut just said that in the time we were talking we crossed realities—hues and somehow I didn't notice. He let me chew on that. It did take me several long moments to process that nifty cosmological piece of trivia.

Then I pointed my finger in the air in a professorial manner. "Ah, but let's say I entered a new hue without knowing it, then how could I have memories that corroborate this new hue? What, did the universe just make it up?"

"Memories, space, time are all part of the consciousness that is existence. It's not any more 'made up' than your thoughts right now. Would you say you're 'concocting' consc . . ."

Helmut snapped his fingers. I wanted to show him this photo of the Jell-O mold I made the night before.

My last will and testament

I wasn't exactly happy with the idea of having to die, even if it was for a good reason. I held on to the hope that the Stubb Foundation would find a hue that would allow me to live. But I also knew it was best to be prepared for the worst. Stacy and I worked out a private arrangement to ensure that the Stubb Foundation honored our agreement should it be necessary for me to take one for the team. But I also needed an official will. The following was copied and pasted from my last will and testament.

If you are reading this, I'm dead. If I died naked, screaming, and covered in blood then we'll call it a draw.

As it stands, I own a 1986 Toyota pickup with a brand new engine and a kick ass stereo system that would blow out the windows of a neighboring car. I own a 1996 Kona Mountain bike. I have numerous CDs and cassettes, the entire series of *The X-Files* on VHS. I have a $300 bed frame from IKEA, two $50 floor lamps from Target, a hand-me-down dresser, my clothes, a collection of coffeehouse T-shirts and my big blue coffee cup. It's not much of an estate. I could donate all of it to Salvation Army but I wanted some personal items bequeathed to my friends and family first.

- The Toyota goes to you, mom
- Jack, you get the bat'leth I made in that blacksmithing class in college. It's still at mom's house.
- Zeke, you remember how you made fun of my shiny new bike? Well, it's yours, fool!

- Stacy, you can have my furniture. I don't think it's cruelty-free, but it's free, so I would take it. You really need something other than those milk crates.
- Gary, you get all of my band T-shirts. I stole them from Ejay, anyway.
- Ejay, you get my music collection of artists starting with a vowel. Artist name doesn't include "the," or "a" in the calculation and if it's a proper name then it's the last name. If it's a fictitious name then it's the first name you go by. Got it?
- Tara, you get my music collection of artists starting with a consonant. Same rules apply.
- Aidan, my dear sponsor, you get my books.
- Meredith, *The X-Files* tapes are yours. Additionally, I want you to have all of my coffeehouse T-shirts. I also want you to have my big blue coffee cup. And here's the logon for my hotmail account: ChubElovr12

My remains: I want to be cremated, and I want the majority of my ashes dumped somewhere in the Barton Creek Greenbelt, preferably at Campbell's Hole. Save a little ash to dump at Flipnotics somewhere. I really loved that coffeehouse.

My funeral: No wailing and beating of chests in anguish, but no jazz funeral either. I want Zeke to pour a 40 on the ground. Ironic considering I'm a recovering alcoholic, I know, but I'm sentimental that way. I want you to play "It's So Hard to Say Goodbye to Yesterday" by Boyz II Men. Isn't that a tad bit cheesy? Yes, get used to it, because at the wake you will listen to the mixtape included in this will of all of my guilty pleasures to include but not limited to Goo Goo Dolls, 2Pac (yes, Zeke, that shit was dope), and a pant load of one-hit wonders from the '80s.

Laugh at my poor taste, make jokes, tell funny stories, touching ones, too if you would like. Have iced coffee (made properly, of course).

About death: I believe in reincarnation, though I wouldn't bet my life on it (insert comedy drum roll). This isn't an optimistic statement. In fact, it's a pain in the ass. If there was nothing after death, then my troubles would be over. Frankly, I just can't buy the concept of heaven and hell after death. Trust me, I would love to believe in it, but I just don't. I suspect that I am going to have to reincarnate repeatedly, live as a man, a woman, an attorney, what not until I can achieve moksha or some non-union/made in China equivalent. But know this: I look forward to working with all of you in the lives to come. And know that I love you all. AMF.

27

Western civilization's cul de sac

Summer 1999

Song being played at the coffeehouse:
"Let Forever Be" by The Chemical Brothers
Visit www.michaeljuge.com on the *Here We Are Now* page to listen

Stacy and I were having coffee at Bouldin Creek Café after our home group AA meeting. Having a regular weekly AA meeting with Stacy was a way to keep my ass in order. I was a bad recovering alcoholic. I didn't go to three or more meetings a week. Hell, sometimes weeks passed between meetings. By the time I found my way into one, I hadn't relapsed or anything so spectacular, but I was certainly a raving asshole by then. Stacy noticed I was beginning to get a little squirrely and it wasn't the impending death thing either. She and I had been a little at odds of late. She was getting increasingly political while I was pining over Meredith to the point of being a nuisance forcing the household to stay off the phone while I was online typing slutty poetry to her. I noticed Stacy had been getting more absorbed in her work at Rapture as well as with her political activities. Going to a meeting every week together was a way for us to both keep our heads in the game and not lose sight of our primary purpose of staying sober. It also had a way of bringing us closer together.

Stacy and Gary had been dating during the spring semester. They kept in touch but he had returned home for the summer to some place in Virginia called Rochelle. He invited us to come up to visit sometime.

"So, you put it somewhere safe?"

Stacy stirred her Vietnamese iced coffee to mix the sweetened condensed milk with the freshly dripped coffee and chicory. "I put the tapes in a safety deposit box. If they don't pay in six months after you . . . you know . . . I'll send it out to every news agency. And I will also upload it onto the web."

"Really? How does that work?"

Stacy smiled. "I'm working on a website where anyone can upload a video and share it publicly. I'm thinking of calling it 'Freedom TV,' 'You Vision,' or something like that. The only problem is the bandwidth requirements are demanding. And a lot of PCs just don't have the video cards necessary."

I didn't catch everything she said, but I got the gist, which was an improvement. I figured Stacy's concept had merit. Perhaps one day people would post videos on the Internet.

"Well, I think the safety deposit box is a good idea. Don't tell me where."

"Oh, I won't."

"But there's something else I think you should do." I didn't know how to broach this touchy subject so I just went into it.

"The Stubb Foundation might anticipate this move, the part of me telling you. They might . . . if they silenced you . . ."

Stacy nodded. "I already considered that as a possibility."

"You did? Gee, you're smart."

"Yeah, thanks. Oh, and thanks for pulling me into your potential web of death."

"Sorry. But seriously, you should also make contingency plans."

"Already taken care of. I told someone what to do upon *my* untimely death."

"Really? Who?"

"Just like the bank, it's best that you don't know."

"Got it."

She looked at her watch. "Well, enough with our deaths, we'd better motor if we're gonna make the show."

Ejay's band Fist Dive was opening for the headliner The Recliners over at Ego's. Fist Dive was a competent ska hop band as ska bands go. Ejay was a talented wordsmith and his funky dreadlocks gave credence to the otherwise all-white band. Stacy and I were happy to show our support for our friend and roommate. But I really came to see The Recliners. They were a lounge act who played snappy, swing renditions of songs like "Welcome to the Jungle" and "Come as You Are." The lead singer Neil wore a frilly tux, went into the audience and asked, "Where are you from," and things like that as they transformed some of rock's hard songs into catchy tunes that the entire family could enjoy.

I sometimes felt as though we had reached a dead end in Western civilization. Well, maybe not a dead end, more like a street that looped around or something. For awhile now, we had seen the way decades went retro. I heard that in the '70s there was a retro '50s thing going. I certainly recalled the retro '60s during the late '80s. The media really pushed the Baby Boomers' decade down Gen X's throat when we were teenagers. It was like they were saying, "See how much more fun we were than you before AIDS and crack, how cool we were back then and how we changed the social landscape? What are you slackers doing?" Between "We Didn't Start the Fire," "Summer of '69" and the litany of movies set in the '60s, I became brainwashed. I was nostalgic over the '60s even though I wasn't born until the '70s. Of course, the Baby Boomers glossed over the spread of STDs and the rise of heroin and cocaine use. They spent a lot of their time focusing on themselves (yeah, pot calling the kettle black, I know), and getting divorced because it "felt good." Wow, is it bitter in here or is it just me?

The '90s were no exception to going retro. We had gone full-throttle into the '70s. The Recliners reflected a small portion of that with lounge acts. They reminded me of Murph and the Magic Tones playing at the Holiday Inn or some backup band to Charo, and that's *exactly* what they were going for! I figured one day, perhaps twenty years in the future, people would go retro '90s. Perhaps they would wear flannel and say things like "the bomb" and "think outside the box."

They might even listen to classic gangsta rap and grunge music. But I bet they'll forget to play disco and wear leisure suits.

But what really made me think while listening to The Recliners play "Back in Black" was that at some point in the future, assuming the universe survives the 26th, we will reference our current retro references. In this not-too-distant future, say twenty years from now, what if by going retro '90s they remember to go retro '70s as well? What will happen to Western civilization then? There's appreciating irony. I understand that. Gen X was the first generation to fully embrace irony. But then there's this new level of referencing the referencing, a self-referential loop, a "meta-reference" if you will. And it was at this moment I had just come up with my master's thesis . . . and it was still summer. Awesome. I'll call it *Irony and Western Civilization's Cul De Sac*. Was it really an anthropology topic? Hell, what in this Anthropology Department was?

28

Porcelain

Summer 1999

I told Meredith about my idea for my thesis. She absolutely loved it, so I knew it was a winner.

Meanwhile, Meredith told me about what she was doing over at the UN. She was supposed to be working on a project to encourage a shift in agricultural techniques in an effort to reduce water consumption in the Golan Heights, something she had done a lot of research on over at the LBJ School. But in typical UN fashion, they decided enough with utilizing these bright young and highly motivated people to further realistic objectives with observable and accountable results. Instead, they put Meredith to work on the Nigerian Commission on Space Exploration.

So, is this commission talking about sending Nigerians into space? I inquired in one of our proto-instant messaging email exchanges.

I could hear her sigh through cyber space.

No. It's a commission of Nigerians discussing the idea of space exploration and its benefit to humanity. I'm so glad they pulled me away from all of that frivolous nonsense with water policy in the Levant. Darn, I wish they had a sarcastic font.

I think I could point this as the moment Meredith became officially jaded. I bet you didn't know this, but Meredith was the one who came up with the ☹ emoticon.

I went to bed each night corresponding with Meredith. Funny thing, but I began to feel as though we were getting to know each other more intimately despite being physically apart. We got to know each other in ways through writing I think would take years to accomplish in person.

Much of my days were spent doing bike-mounted deliveries downtown. I wondered if Helmut planned to have someone do a hit-and-run on me, so I told him that I was on to him if that's what he was indeed planning. He seemed legitimately hurt by the implication and reassured me that I would go out with notification and it would be quick and I wouldn't even feel it.

When I wasn't at the Stubb Foundation, I was hanging with the Lord of the Flies crew in the copy room over at the Law Office of Taylor, Swift and Lavigne. You would think that after work I would be happy to go home to rest, and watch some Comedy Central. But I had a lot of energy. Perhaps it had to do with knowing my life was in a precarious position. That or it was the lack of sex. Either way, I was antsy after work, so I did a lot of mountain biking in the Greenbelt. Moby summer had me making the most of my time. I have to say, for someone who loved television, I wasn't doing a lot of TV watching.

Meredith encouraged me to go to the library and get myself learned up on this computer thing. I got books on *Microsoft Office for Dummies*, and *Sock Puppet Explanations* for the current state of home use PCs. Something I had always avoided and feared became less intimidating once I understood the basics. I started to experiment with various applications and found it wasn't really all that complicated. And for the most part, whenever something went wrong, it wasn't my fault, it was simply the PC freezing up, because Microsoft Windows really sucked back then. Everyone had problems with their computers crashing, not just me. That was reassuring.

We held parties at the Travis Heights house as we always had. Raquel's rejects would spin tales of this mysterious, larger-than-life character who was now, according to us, an assassin for the Mossad hunting down future Nazis while opening fried chicken franchises throughout Eastern Europe. We were running out of ideas. This one particular party we were celebrating the US Women's soccer team victory over China for the World Cup. Ejay, Tara and I had finished our tales, Gary had flown into town to sign the lease for a new apartment and was spinning a fusion between Britney Spears and Tool, Stacy and Zeke were arguing over Mexican restaurants (Stacy was at a disadvantage to one Ezequiel Luevano-Hernandez), and Cliff and Reagan were throwing cans of beer at each other. I took in the scene around me and I felt something. No, it wasn't déjà vu. It was one of those moments I was telling you about. I knew this was a moment in time. Whether the universe survived or not, this moment was a precious, fleeting moment. Sublime impermanence.

I turned to Ejay and Tara. "I think I'm getting nostalgic."

Tara scoffed. "For what? The '80s?"

I smiled. "No. I'm nostalgic for right now. This moment here. I just know that one day, I'm going to look back and I'm going to get nostalgic for this period in my life. I'm going to remember this very party and I will think of you and remember how we were close. I'm going to get nostalgic about this strange time in my life, this period when I didn't know what lay ahead of me, when I was lost, but it was okay because we were all lost together. So, I figure, why wait? I'm going to get nostalgic about now right now."

Ejay put his hand on my shoulder and gave me a hug. It was really sweet. It was followed by a massive burp in my face. And with that the moment of sublime impermanence had passed.

As Ice Cube said, "Today was a good day. I didn't even have to use my A.K." I went to work, made the cocoa for the staff at the Stubb Foundation as they woke from their slumber. They were all now sleeping together in the living area where they tied their mattresses together. Maybe they did freaky things at night when I left; I didn't dwell on it. I was in my cat's cradle corner sorting through their mail when Helmut came up. He was holding a mug of cocoa and supported himself against a wall casually.

"Hey, Chris, what's happening." I couldn't tell if he was referencing *Office Space* or if he was just being himself. The entire city of Austin was referencing that movie. It didn't matter, because he casually added, "Um yeah, about that whole possibly having to die thing, don't worry about it. We found another hue."

I froze. I couldn't believe it. Did he just say what I thought he said? I was almost too scared to confirm, but I had to. "You mean . . . I don't have to die?"

"That's right. We found another hue that will be much more conducive."

"So, I'm off the hook?"

"Yeah, looks like it. I still need you to operate the device on the 26th. You are the Chris after all."

I jumped up and gave Helmut a bear hug, spilling his cocoa on him. I proceeded to bounce with him in my arms.

"Okay, okay, Chris. I'm getting a little nauseous now."

"Oh, sorry about that. Oh, and sorry about your shirt, too."

"Meh, don't worry. It was the time of the month to change it anyway."

Sadly, he wasn't being facetious.

Song on my mixtape of guilty pleasures:
"Name" by Goo Goo Dolls
Visit www.michaeljuge.com on the *Here We Are Now* page to listen

There is nothing more life-affirming that having the sword of Damocles removed from over your head. I bought the entire Stubb foundation lunch and paid for the weekend's supply of Hot Pockets myself. I was already running up my credit card thinking I could pull a fast one by dying on them. I might as well tap it out by getting my saviors a free lunch. I dropped by CynerDygm to do deliveries during their weekly beer bash and I informed Stacy that she could stand down. She was relieved. I noticed this week's beer bash at CynerDygm was especially festive and extravagant. Word had it that they were going to be purchased by Dell after having been a "third round" for over a year. Nothing solid, but the elderly 40-year-old CEO was out there with the employees doing the robot.

After work I went cycling into the Greenbelt as I always did. I had become quite adept on my Kona. I was able to hop up rocks that I couldn't when I first moved to Austin. I was able to push through rocky climbs and no longer feared making jumps from boulder to boulder. I was a passable mountain biker now. I rode along the rocky paths beside Barton Creek, passing by rock climbers and hippies with their dogs underneath the cliffs hanging above. As long as I lived in Austin, I never tired of its beauty. I rode back home up the hill on South Congress into the Travis Heights neighborhood and up the final stretch to my house at the crest. And there I saw the Toyota Corolla.

"No," I whispered to myself. It couldn't be. I didn't want to get my hopes up, but what control did I have of my emotions?

As I jumped off my Kona, I saw her sitting on the front steps. Meredith Anderson, the most beautiful woman, stood up and sauntered over to me dressed in summer shorts and sandals. I dropped my bike and threw off my helmet. I strode up to her and stopped. I had been cycling hard and was covered in sweat. I didn't want to offend. But she was here!

"I . . . you weren't supposed to come till next week," I croaked. My mouth was dry.

Meredith brushed her reddish brunette hair from her face and smiled. "The UN will survive."

"I missed you." I held back the tears as best I could. I didn't want to break down, but it had been a big day, you understand. Meredith caressed my face with her hand.

"Can I tell you a secret?" she said. "That day when I left Pangaea and accidentally bumped into you at Mojo's when I said I was heading to Half Price Books."

"Yeah?"

"It wasn't an accident me bumping into you."

I quirked my head a little and then realized she had pulled the old accidental bump into you routine just as I had done to her.

I took her hand. "Meredith . . . I, um, I . . ."

"And I love you, Chris Jung."

Suffice it to say "Porcelain" was played a lot that night. There was no better way to wrap up Moby Summer.

29

Going out on a school night

Tuesday evening, October 26, 1999

Scariest movie: *The Blair Witch Project*
The last legitimate thing MTV showed: The video to "Praise You" by
Fatboy Slim

For the rest of the world it was another Tuesday evening. Stacy was
hosting another Greens meeting. They were talking about going to
some big WTO protest next month in Seattle. I hoped they would be
around to get to do that. I didn't care about the politics that much. I
just wanted there to be protestors, cops, WTO, IMF and everybody
else in this screwed-up world in this imperfect universe in November
and beyond. Tara was making adjustments to Hillary for the upcoming
robot war and brought Hillary home to test the stairs. Ejay was making
an Indian dish with his new girlfriend, an actual girlfriend, not just
a hookup. Meredith and I were sitting in bed reading our semester's
worth of books while I got distracted by the NBC made-for-TV movie
about Y2K and the end of the world.

It was just another school night in the little backwoods corner in
the Milky Way galaxy, home to a perpetually angry species of nuclear-
age primates. At some point I turned off the TV so that Meredith and I
could take a nap break. I turned out the lights and we lay down listening
to the wind rustling the leaves.

"It's like living in a tree house," she whispered. She was right. We were perched up into the trees and the windows on all three sides made it seem as though this room was nestled in the crook of one of the larger branches.

Lying down, my eyes were wide open. I was tired but there was no way I could doze off, not with the fate of all existence to be decided in the next few hours. I was going to be instrumental in determining our collective fate—no pressure. I resigned myself to not discussing this with Meredith. I couldn't say how she would respond and there was just too much at stake. I believe they called that thoughtful reticence "discretion," something else I learned from the same woman I was withholding vital information from, ironically enough. I wished I had that discretion a year ago before blabbering off to my roommates. That being said, there were a host of other thoughts coursing through my mind.

"You ever wonder if you were ever meant to do something, like, you were born for a particular purpose?"

Meredith took a moment before answering. "I think we all wonder that. I know I ask myself whether there is intrinsic meaning to our existence. And if purpose is derived from that."

"There are people who know what they are meant to do. They knew from the time they were born. I never had a clue. I didn't have a passion. My siblings knew what they wanted. Those people at those startups where I do my deliveries, they tell me that they're changing the world. Maybe they are. I don't know. They know what they were meant to do."

The next few hours would decide whether all of this ever mattered. All the pain and suffering humanity had endured, the hope for the future, it would either be remembered or it would not have ever been. And despite something so fundamental, I was struck by my own selfish thoughts. *And what about you, Chris?* If the universe is to continue to chug along, will I continue to do what I have been doing my whole life—wander aimlessly, backing my way into a life pattern? I didn't know what my best destiny was, what I was meant to do unlike the Stubb Foundation members. I just floated in the breeze and found myself somewhere. Hell, it's how I wound up in Austin; it's how I wound up at UT. I grant that all of those half-baked decisions brought me to sharing a bed with Meredith. Without a doubt, this has been the highlight of my life. And yet, I couldn't help but feel that I was missing something, and it was my fault.

"I . . . I just want to know what I am supposed to do." *Is this why I got sober?* I asked myself that a lot.

"Chris, it isn't about jobs, money, or finding spiritual enlightenment in some silly startup. It's about becoming the man you always wanted to be whatever you do to pay the rent. It's staying true to him that counts."

Helmut called my cell phone and I rushed to answer it before it would wake Meredith up.

"You're not asleep are you?" Helmut inquired.

I whispered back. "No. Of course not." I would have thought it impossible, but indeed I had dozed off.

"Okay, well, I think it's time you head out. You have the directions?"

"Got them right here." Helmut had provided me with a Mapquest printout this morning when he dropped off the device at my house.

"I've included instructions how to work the device but the AI should be able to handle it automatically once you plug it in."

AI. That means artificial intelligence. That's what Helmut and the rest of the Stubb Foundation came to call the organic CPU made of orange goo. I thought it odd that Helmut went through the trouble of dropping off the device and the AI at my house. I was their courier, after all. But he was insistent that I not show up at work today. He explained the crew was too engaged to be interrupted.

"I still think you should come with me, Helmut. I might screw this up."

"You won't. You're the Chris. Just follow the instructions. Good luck." He hung up.

I left the house with Meredith sound asleep in my room, cuddled with a copy of *Emerging Markets and Infrastructure in the New Economy.* Just in case, I left a note saying I went to the store to get some shampoo.

It was factually true. I drove *Value Menus* an hour south of Austin to an outer suburb of San Antonio, a town named Universal City, significantly enough. I took the exit and drove past a small airbase and into blackness. And there, in the middle of nowhere beyond the edge of the metropolitan area along the highway, I found a Target store where I was supposed to go. Texas did weird things like building stuff way out in the middle of nowhere expecting people to just show up. Funny thing was, they usually did. I figured in ten years this Target store would be surrounded by a Petsmart and a Tinseltown movie theater, which would likewise be surrounded by a bunch of desperate suburbanistans.

It was a little past 11 p.m. when I arrived, so it was a little surprising to find this brand new Target store open, as it was set out in the middle of nowhere. And yet it was, just as Helmut said it would be. I looked for the spot in the empty parking lot and found the spray-painted symbol of the Stubb Foundation where I was supposed to park. I jogged part of the way from the parking lot to the store, moving somewhat hurriedly from the darkness towards the light-source of the Target store. I think having seen *The Blair Witch Project* the previous weekend with Meredith had something to do with it. I'm not ashamed to say that movie scared the shit out of me. That part at the end where you see Michael facing the wall . . . Dude. As the doors slid open, one of the clerks called out on the intercom, "He's here."

I gave her a look and the lady said, "Come on. Do your thing." I realized the Stubb Foundation had pulled some strings with this store and convinced them to stay open for me. I felt a little self—conscious, but looking at my watch I didn't have time to ponder. I took a basket and searched for the items on the list.

I bought two bottles of Head and Shoulders shampoo (just as it said I was to do in the note) and a bottle of Pantene conditioner for damaged hair, the one where you stand it up on its cap. Helmut was specific. I then bought the generic brand box of tampons and a bag of cat litter. There was one register open with the grumpy store clerk. She checked my items. I paid in cash per the instructions. As I started heading for the doors, I noticed the employees turning off the lights and closing down the cash register. By the time I was outside, they had closed the store.

I walked back to *Value Menus* where I set up the AI and hooked it to a device the Stubb Foundation put together. Helmut had given me instructions, but I had already committed the entire procedure to memory. I didn't want to screw it up. I turned on *Value Menus'* engine and powered up this strange-looking device by connecting jumper cables to the rods protruding from it. The device looked a lot like just another sub woofer with nodes. I then powered the AI with the organic CPU by connecting it to the cigarette lighter. The orange goo glowed to life. I then used a USB cable (I knew to call it that by now) to connect the CPU with the device. I looked at my watch: 11:31. I waited for a minute before I smacked myself.

"Shit, I almost forgot," I yelled into the night.

I took the auxiliary audio cable, plugged it into an output that Helmut had custom made from the car stereo receiver and connected it to the device's input jack. At 11:33 I selected the song on the CD changer.

As instructed, at 11:33, "November Rain" played.

So many things could go wrong. What if I didn't buy the right tampons? He said "generic," but what if that was the name of the brand? What if I started the CD a millisecond too early or late? What if there's a scratch on the CD? Did I remember to pay cash? *Yes, yes I did. Well, what about the . . .*

And then *Value Menus* started to shake as the philharmonic orchestra was accompanied by the drums. As Axl began to sing, I felt a strong gust of wind. The goo in the AI started vibrating several hues, flickering like a strobe out of sync. The wind changed directions and I could feel it now moving upward. I looked up and saw a funnel formation of clouds in the sky. I turned the volume up just to be sure. The wind got louder and I heard a whirling sound. *Value Menus* shimmied and the engine started revving. The windshield suddenly cracked when the song reached the crescendo. Afraid, I stepped out of *Value Menus* and my foot landed onto . . . not ground. Instead, I fell into an abyss.

I can't explain what exactly what it all meant, but this is what I saw next.

I was picking up a six-year sobriety chip.

I was slumped in a bar, drunk, a bar I recognized in New Orleans called Miss Mae's.

I saw Meredith smiling.

I was in a suit covered in soot and I was running from a plume of smoke.

I saw blackness.

There were people I didn't recognize around me.

I saw myself inside an understand train station, and I could feel what I was feeling at that moment; complete utter despair. I was stepping over the edge as the lights of a train approached.

I saw myself crying in Meredith's arms.

I saw a man dressed in battle fatigues riding a bicycle, of all things.

I saw myself holding a baby and feeling the most tender feelings I ever felt. I never felt so vulnerable in my life holding this boy, a baby boy, my son.

I saw Meredith and I arguing.

I saw protests

I saw myself working inside a cubicle looking at a website.

I saw Meredith taking my hand as we witnessed our daughter getting married. I knew she was our daughter.

I saw myself roughly forty pounds heavier, sitting in my old room at my mom's house playing a video game with really sophisticated graphics where other players joined online.

I was teaching my son to play baseball, though I didn't know anything about baseball.

I was hammering in a blacksmith's shop.

I was typing a report on a computer where the screen was paper-thin.

I saw Meredith older, but somehow she seemed the same to me.

I was holding her wrinkled hand as she stood over me, and I never felt so at home, and I desperately wanted to stay with her, stay in this moment, this fleeting moment forever, but I also wanted to rest. I was so tired. And she said I can rest now. And I . . .

I came to with the violent sound of shrieking metal. I had apparently fallen onto the pavement, and with a massive headache I stood up. *Value*

Menus swayed and jumped like it had hydraulics. The shrieking metal sound increased and, suddenly, the truck bed crumpled onto itself as if being crushed by an invisible compactor. Glass shattered.

I scurried away and cursed, "Shit! My truck!" *Value Menus* collapsed on itself the way a house built on an Indian burial ground would. I watched as my pickup crumpled, getting smaller and smaller, the noise was getting deafening.

And then as the noise peaked in intensity it suddenly went all quiet. *Value Menus* was gone. The wind still blew, but it was a pleasant breeze now, nothing ominous. The funnel above had disappeared to be replaced by gentle clouds meetings stars in the night sky. I cautiously approached the spot where *Value Menus* had been and was glad to see that indeed there was a parking spot. There was a shopping cart stall. I turned around to see that the Target store was still there. I looked at my watch. It was 12:03 a.m., October, 27th. I, and apparently the rest of the universe, were still here. It worked. They succeeded. The Stubb Foundation saved the universe.

And after witnessing the most significant event in the history of the universe since the big bang, my next thought was trying to figure how I was going to get home. I started walking towards the now-closed Target store. Maybe the clerk or one of the other employees would be so kind as to drop me off at a bus station or something. I couldn't believe it. For so long, I had built up this moment of where the fate of the universe would be decided. Shouldn't I feel something, some awesome catharsis or anything? But alas, I just wanted to go home.

Song that inexplicably played in my head:
"Cast No Shadow" by Oasis
Visit www.michaeljuge.com on the *Here We Are Now* page to listen

In the distance I saw a red Saab parked by the loading dock with a figure standing beside it. The long-haired man was lanky and had a scraggly beard.

"Helmut?" It was him all right. I jogged over to meet him.

"So, we did it, didn't we?" I asked. This wasn't entirely rhetorical. I wanted to be sure it worked.

Helmut nodded stoically. "Yes, Chris. We succeeded. The rift has been sealed. There is a hue where it did swallow existence, for infinite hues require that, but it is contained."

"Awesome. Man, I was thinking how crazy it was that in all of the universe the strongest point to combat the Absence would be here outside a Target."

"The fabric of space/time has more potential for both disruption as well as strengthening near a large Hadron collider. And that is why I had Texas A&M work with the US government to build one just over that fence there."

"What's a large Hadron collider?"

"It's not important. But we curved the hues so that we could build what we needed to build and attract the Absence while simultaneously sealing it within a hue. All of those companies, those consortiums and government officials and startups played a part in saving the universe. They just don't know it."

"Cool. Well, I think there's a Whataburger near the interstate entrance. I'm feeling hungry. Aren't you? I'll need a ride of course. Hey, did you see what it did to *Value Menus*?"

"Yeah, sorry about that."

"Meh, cost of doing business I suppose. I will be requesting compensation, though. I'll come by work tomorrow . . ."

"No!" Helmut turned to me and clasped my shoulders. "Listen to me, Chris. You must not return to the Stubb Foundation. Do not return there," he commanded.

I stared at him. "Why can't I return to the Stubb Foundation?"

I saw the conflict within him. And then it occurred to me. I hesitated before asking, "What happened, Helmut?"

He folded his arms protectively. "It was the only way."

"What was?"

"Sheila. She figured how to save you. She found the hue that would allow you to live and to contain the Absence, but it came at a cost." He paused trembling. "Twenty of us would have to sacrifice ourselves in order to bring us to this hue."

My mouth opened. I wanted to speak, but no words came out.

"It was the only way, Chris. They knew this and they volunteered to die."

"No." I started to feel sick as I staggered back. "I didn't ask them to kill themselves for me. I didn't ask anyone to do that!"

"I know, Chris. I know. You were willing to have your own life taken. But Sheila and the others wanted to find another way. They all were amenable to returning to the sea."

"All of them? You said only twenty had to do it. Why all of them?"

"They think collectively. And none of them could handle being on their own. Besides, it was what they were meant to do. It was what they were born to do. Surely, you could appreciate that."

Intellectually, I knew what he said made sense. That was their purpose, after all, and I had always looked for purpose in *my* life. But as a person I couldn't accept a mass suicide being just part of the nature of things.

He whispered. "They liked you, and they realized that you are needed here more than they."

"Me . . . needed? For what? To deliver more shit to law offices and startups? To finish my thesis?" I spat out sarcastically. "Why is it more important that one mope lives while twenty-three souls perish? Where's the sense in that?"

"They were ready to return to the sea of consciousness that we are all part of and that you cannot even come close to perceiving. Besides, you are needed here."

"Why? Why am I supposed to live? What for, Helmut?"

"You will be needed for something one day."

I paused. "Are you . . . are you saying I do have a purpose, something beyond this?" I wanted to know. It's what I always wanted to know. "Tell me, Helmut. Please."

"I'm sorry. I can't say anything more than that."

Helmut wouldn't budge. Whatever I was meant to do one day I would just have to discover it on my own. So, we stood there. The doors from Target slid open as the clerk came out and started locking the doors down.

Helmut extended his hand holding a set of keys. "The Saab is yours. I filled it up. You purchased it from me months ago in this hue."

"Wait. We're in a different hue, now?"

"It's basically the same, just one where you never worked for us." I took the keys from him. I couldn't process what had just happened, much less the idea of being transported to a slightly alternate reality.

"Don't you need a ride or something?" As I said that, the clerk pulled her Ford pickup up to the two of us. Helmut gestured to the clerk in the pickup.

"I got a ride."

"Where are you going?"

"It's not important. It was a pleasure knowing you. Have an awesome life, Chris Jung."

"And you, too, Helmut Spankmeister." We hugged and he jumped into the clerk's truck. They drove off into the night, receding into the distance leaving me alone in the darkened Target store parking lot. I climbed slowly into the red Saab recognizing items that were clearly mine to include the big blue coffee cup. It was as though I really had been driving this car for months. As I started the engine, the car stereo came to life. It was playing "Cast No Shadow."

The obligatory epilogue: The end of the '90s

The local and national news outlets reported a mass suicide at an obscure dotcom in South Austin. The cameras showed how the "cult members" of the Stubb Foundation tied all of their mattresses together and consumed a lethal cocktail. It wasn't really Kool-Aid, but it didn't matter. Everyone made the reference anyway. The media intimated that the foundation members lived in a constant state of orgies and Hot Pockets. I stared at the TV screen and saw the images of the bodies being pulled out from the concrete mansion off of Barton Springs. I broke down and sobbed. Sheila, Stella, Hank, Siobahn, Hector, Hennessy, Shawna, Harold, Samantha, Heath, all of them. I expected the cops to show up to interview me. But none came. As Helmut told me before driving off with the store clerk into the night, I existed in a hue where I had neither ever been assigned there by Logos, nor had I ever been employed by the Stubb Foundation part time when I started grad school. None of my friends made any connection to me working there, either. Ejay had no snarky comment about *The Neverending Story* or me being "the Chris," for in this hue I never told my roommates any such ridiculous story. There was no mention of a missing member, namely Helmut Spankmeister. According to the news, the entire staff of twenty-*three* members were dead, not twenty-four. I cried seeing the images flash on the television. Meredith asked if I knew any of them. We were an item in this hue as well as the previous one, much to my relief. I couldn't mention my involvement in the other hue to anyone. I certainly couldn't explain why I remembered a different hue from the one that I was in. The term itself meant nothing here. I did the only thing I could do: try to put it behind me.

December 31, 1999

Song on my mixtape lamenting the end of an era:
"Crash Into Me" by Dave Matthews
Visit www.michaeljuge.com on the *Here We Are Now* page to listen

The nasty business with the mass suicide at the Stubb Foundation had been completely forgotten by the general public by New Year's Eve. In the final days of 1999, the world was both freaking out and celebrating the arrival of 2000, the unofficial turn of the millennium. Y2K was pushing the survivalists to DEFCON 1 while the rest of the world was preparing for an epic party that would make the last turn of the millennium look like a turd in comparison. Of course, it was not fair to compare this one to the last. They didn't even have plumbing yet, much less Will Smith to party with.

Meredith, Ejay, Tara, Gary, Zeke and Laura (now commonly referred to as "Zaura"), and I were in New Orleans to celebrate the new year. Stacy was stuck back in Austin at CynerDygm running final tests to ensure that the computers were ready for Y2K; poor woman. My mom was happy to meet the much-talked-about Meredith in person, and I introduced Meredith to my sponsor Aidan, the grizzled Vietnam veteran. It was good to see him again, but I could tell that he was not doing well physically. During New Year's Eve day we went to a jazz funeral for the 20th century. As evening approached we all headed to the French Quarter and I got wired on a PJs coffee granita.

As the hours drew closer to midnight, I felt a mixture of excitement and sorrow. I had pushed the Stubb Foundation out of my active consciousness for the most part, so it wasn't that. I felt sad about saying goodbye to the 1900s. I mean, how stupid is that? I had been feeling down the entire day about it, though. This was the last day ever in the history of everything where I would be here in the 1900s. The members of the Stubb Foundation (may their consciousness be swimming in the sea now) saw time and space as a jiggling Jell-O mold that you could slurp around with a straw, but I was tied to one hue, and to one direction in time. The 1900s and, more to the point, the 1990s were about to cease to be real. I would never be here in the '90s again. In effect, the '90s were dying. As silly as it sounds, that was exactly how I saw it. I don't know. I guess I listened to too much Morrissey as a teenager, and it completely messed up my perspective.

But in all fairness, the '90s had been my decade. It was the decade I got sober. It was the decade I found my best friend Stacy. It was the decade I nutted up, took matters into my own hands and the decade where I made a city my own. Remember how a few months ago during the summer I told Tara, Stacy and Ejay how I was nostalgic for that moment we were in? I guess I was experiencing a pre-emptive nostalgia now, because I knew one day I would look back at this period in my life and long to visit it again, if ever so briefly, just to say "hi."

We all staged at The Dragon's Den on Esplanade, where my brother Jack and his friends at subVerse came to town and rented the restaurant for a ridiculous sum. Meredith pulled me out of my funk the moment I saw her walk out of the dressing room. The shimmering red and black cocktail dress and pumps would put wood into Morrissey himself. As we headed down Decatur to see the ball descend at Jackson Square, Meredith took my hand, partially for support. New Orleans streets are hell on heels. I can't tell you how many times I saw punk girls in thigh-length, high-heeled patent leather boots wipe out on the treacherous sidewalks trying to get from Molly's at the Market to The Avalon. There's nothing sadder than seeing a punk rock girl with scuffed-up leather.

"You've been quiet!" Meredith screamed above the din. We were in the middle of the packed street, the churning crowd made conversation nearly impossible.

"Ah, just thinking!"

"Uh-oh," she said. "Let's keep that to a mimimum . . . I mean, min . . . imim!" and then she giggled in the most infectious way. At most, Meredith had one glass of wine and a Kahlua drink with dinner, but she was flying. She was a cheap date, to be certain. I wondered if that was a Wisconsin thing.

I smiled and put my arm around her waist. I didn't know if we would last. I sure as hell hoped so. Meredith was everything I ever wanted before I knew what I wanted. I hoped I would get a job, a real job. Everything was up for grabs, but I guess that was part of the deal with being human. The '90s was a pivotal decade for me to be sure, but it was just a moment in time. It was time to let go and embrace what I feared . . . the unknown.

Throughout the French Quarter, the crowd started their countdown. "10 . . . 9 . . . 8"

I didn't know what purpose Helmut was referring to that I would fulfill in the future. I still didn't know what the hell to do with the life I had. But one thing I knew was that I had the freedom to choose which hue to go down. That Venetian crème-induced vision could have happened, but it didn't, and I no longer feared it would. As directionless as I was, I also knew to not fear the journey anymore.

Meredith pulled herself close to me. Her reddish-brown hair, slightly out of place from the wind matted to the perspiration on her skin.

"Well, it's coming! Here we are!" she exulted.

"5 . . . 4 . . ."

And I realized again how it was just those moments that mattered the most.

"3 . . . 2 . . ."

I held Meredith close. "Yes, here we are now."

As the credits role by: "Changes" by 2Pac
Visit **www.michaeljuge.com** on the *Here We Are Now* page to listen

About the Author

Michael Juge grew up in New Orleans bumming around aimlessly until he was struck with sobriety. Upon receiving his bachelor's degree in Religious Studies at Loyola University New Orleans, Michael moved to Austin, Texas to find himself. When he found himself to be a courier and barista, he retreated to grad school and obtained his master's degree in Middle Eastern Studies at the University of Texas at Austin. After being saturated with weapons-grade coffee and postmodern cultural theory, Michael went on to something completely different—to serve in the U.S. Department of State. Michael now lives in Texas with his beautiful wife and two kids, where he wanders Central Texas in search of coffeehouse T-shirts. Psychiatrists agree that Michael is harmless.